Restless, Jessica got up and walked back inside, standing right next to the patio door. Who would she want to talk to if her only family member were in the hospital?

She pressed her head against the window, the glass feeling cold and sticky against her forehead.

It was an easy answer. But could she really do that? Could she push the person who mattered most to her toward Jade *again*, even after the way Jade had treated her today?

Get over yourself. This was serious. The girl's mother was in the hospital. And he—for whatever reason—really cared about Jade. He'd want to know if she was in trouble.

Before she could change her mind, she went into the kitchen and picked up the phone, then dialed Jeremy's number.

Don't miss any of the books in SWEET VALLEY HIGH
SENIOR YEAR, an exciting series from Bantam Books!

#1 CAN'T STAY AWAY

#2 SAY IT TO MY FACE

#3 SO COOL

#4 I'VE GOT A SECRET

#5 IF YOU ONLY KNEW

#6 YOUR BASIC NIGHTMARE

#7 BOY MEETS GIRL

#8 MARIA WHO?

#9 THE ONE THAT GOT AWAY

#10 BROKEN ANGEL

#11 TAKE ME ON

#12 BAD GIRL

#13 ALL ABOUT LOVE

#14 SPLIT DECISION

#15 ON MY OWN

#16 THREE GIRLS AND A GUY

#17 BACKSTABBER

#18 AS IF I CARE

#19 IT'S MY LIFE

#20 NOTHING IS FOREVER

#21 THE IT GUY

#22 SO NOT ME

#23 FALLING APART

#24 NEVER LET GO

Visit the Official Sweet Valley Web Site on the Internet at:

www.sweetvalley.com

Francine Pascal's SVH senioryear

Never Let Go

CREATED BY
FRANCINE PASCAL

BANTAM BOOKS
NEW YORK • TORONTO • LONDON • SYDNEY • AUCKLAND

RL: 6, AGES 012 AND UP

NEVER LET GO

A Bantam Book / December 2000

Sweet Valley High® is a registered trademark of Francine Pascal.
Conceived by Francine Pascal.
Cover photography by Michael Segal.

Produced by 17th Street Productions,
an Alloy Online, Inc. company.
33 West 17th Street
New York, NY 10011.

ISBN: 0-553-49340-X

Visit us on the Web! www.randomhouse.com/teens

Published simultaneously in the United States and Canada

Bantam Books is an imprint of Random House Children's Books, a
division of Random House, Inc. BANTAM BOOKS and the rooster
colophon are registered trademarks of Random House, Inc. Bantam Books,
1540 Broadway, New York, New York 10036.

PRINTED IN THE UNITED STATES OF AMERICA

OPM   0 9 8 7 6 5 4 3 2 1

To Richard Wenk

Jessica Wakefield

Homecoming dance, senior year.

My big night.

Or at least the night I'd been dreaming would be big ever since seventh grade. Only I imagined it a little differently — like, I'd actually have a date.

I guess it was okay. Hanging out with Tia and Andy was fun. But watching Jeremy stare at Jade like a little puppy dog while she danced with a million other guys? Definitely not fun. So why did it suddenly seem like the most important thing in the world to convince him to work things out with her?

Jeremy Aames

*Why was Jessica so determined to
get me and Jade together last night?
Why is it bugging me so much that she
was?*

Melissa Fox

I still can't believe I went to the homecoming dance last night—without Will.

Everything was going to be perfect this year. I had our outfits picked out months ago.

I was going to have a new picture to replace the one from homecoming last year at El Carro. The one facing me on my dresser right now . . .

But there I was last night, dancing with Ken.

It's still impossible to imagine my future without Will. But I can't imagine it with him either. I mean, if Will doesn't care about anything anymore, does that mean I have to throw away my life too? I don't think so.

And it's not like I went behind his back last night. Well, I didn't exactly tell him I was going with Ken—but I didn't lie to him. How could I? He won't even talk to me.

Ken Matthews

This is it. Homecoming. The biggest game of my senior year. The crowd will be yelling their heads off. The cheerleaders will be going nuts. Cheerleaders. Melissa.

Why can't I get her out of my head? The way she looked last night, the way she smelled . . .

But I can't stop thinking about Maria either and this stupid, crazy wish that she'll show up today and finally be able to be happy for me. Like that would ever happen. She's made it very clear what she thinks of me now.

What I really don't get is that Maria was the one who pushed me to take back my life. Then when I finally got where I wanted to be, she turned around and walked away.

Which is why I have to forget about her and focus on what matters. Focus on the game today. The only people I need in my life are the ones who care about what _I_ care about.

CHAPTER 1
Absolute Freedom

Elizabeth Wakefield stretched her arms over her head and nestled back into her cozy, dark blue sheets. A fuzzy, warm feeling filled her body as she slowly opened her eyes.

She yawned. Where was the crushing feeling of heaviness she was used to waking up to? Normally she was lucky to get in one free, relaxed breath before remembering everything going on with Conner. But it wasn't Conner she was thinking about. It was . . .

Elizabeth sat up, a fistful of white comforter clutched in her hand. Had she really kissed Evan Plummer last night? Right in the middle of the dance floor? In front of basically the entire student body of Sweet Valley High—including her sister?

She flopped back down and pulled the comforter over her head. Jessica was already annoyed at her. What would she say now?

For a second Elizabeth blocked out the image of her angry twin and focused instead on the memory of the kiss. There was a reason she'd woken up happy. Being with Evan last night had been so natural—so comfortable. She'd slept better than she had in weeks.

But still, there were all kinds of questions she had to face now. And not just from other people either. Kissing Evan had been wonderful, but was it really what she wanted? Was he?

She got out of bed and jammed her feet into her slippers. Maybe a shower would clear her head. She grabbed her robe from the closet and knocked on the bathroom door.

There was a pause, then Jessica grumbled a low, "Come in."

Elizabeth bit her lip, then slowly opened the door. Jessica was already dressed in her cheerleader uniform, putting the finishing touches on her makeup. "I'm almost done," she said, without turning away from the mirror. She swiped the eyeliner pencil across her lid, then capped it and spun around. "There. All yours," she said as she passed by.

"Jess?" Elizabeth called after her. "Can I talk to you for a sec?"

Jessica paused in the doorway, her back stiffening. "I'm kind of in a hurry," she said. "I have to get to the homecoming game."

Was she being paranoid, or had Jessica put extra emphasis on the word *homecoming*? Elizabeth shook her head.

"About last night," she began awkwardly. "I . . ." She trailed off as her sister finally faced her with a serious glare. "I need some advice," she forced herself to finish.

"I told you what I think already, and it didn't make much difference, did it?" Jessica said. She flipped her damp hair out of her eyes. "You're just going to do what you want anyway, so what's the point of asking me?" She turned and walked back into her bedroom.

You knew she would be mad, Elizabeth thought, swallowing hard. At least Jessica wasn't freaking out on her. With a deep breath, she followed her sister into her room.

"See, that's the problem," Elizabeth explained as Jessica opened her closet and started fishing around inside. "I don't know what I want. What if I made a big mistake?"

Jessica let out a sharp laugh. She spun around to face Elizabeth. "You, make a mistake?" she said sarcastically. "Oh, Liz, that could *never* happen."

Elizabeth flinched. She'd thought she and Jessica were way past the whole Little-Miss-Perfect-reputation thing. But lately they didn't seem to be past much of anything.

"What do you want me to say?" Jessica yanked her red-and-white letter jacket from the closet. "You don't need my permission if you decide to go after Evan. But I'm really not going to tell you to go for it. I mean, you're the one who kept telling me last week that this has nothing to do with me, remember?"

Elizabeth sighed. She leaned back against the door, pulling her robe tighter around her. Jessica obviously wasn't going to help—she was still hung up on this crazy idea that Elizabeth was "stealing" Evan since he'd dated Jessica for about two seconds a long time ago.

"Look, I have to go to the game," Jessica said. "The bathroom's all yours," she added, waving her hand toward the door. Then she paused, staring closely at Elizabeth. "I just think this whole thing is kind of funny," she said. "When I jumped into things with Evan, you said I needed to take time and make sure I was over Will. Exactly how many days has it been since you broke up with Conner?"

Before Elizabeth could respond, Jessica breezed out of the room. Her footsteps pounded down the stairs, and then everything was quiet.

Elizabeth glanced around her sister's bedroom, feeling strangely helpless. Then she spotted the cordless phone sitting on Jessica's desk. She walked over and grabbed it, then dialed Tia's number. At least Tia had gotten over their stupid fight about Evan. Maybe she could offer some advice.

"Hello?" Tia answered on the second ring, sounding out of breath.

"Hi, Tee," Elizabeth said. "Got a minute?"

"Actually, I'm running out the door. The game, remember? Aren't you going?"

Elizabeth blinked. For a second she'd forgotten

that Tia was captain of the cheerleading squad. If Jessica had been in a hurry, then Tia would be on her way out too.

"I don't think I'm up to it," Elizabeth said, flopping down on Jessica's desk chair. "I'm, um, kind of messed up about what happened last night."

She paused, wondering if Tia would know what she meant. Just how many people *had* witnessed her and Evan's very public kiss?

"Yeah—I was kind of wondering about that," Tia said.

"So you saw us," Elizabeth said with a sigh. "I guess everybody did." There went her last chance for dignity. Elizabeth Wakefield, formerly known as the superconservative prude, had finally managed to wipe clean that image for good!

"I was a little . . . surprised," Tia said carefully. "But Jessica really didn't take it well. Have you talked to her this morning?"

"Yeah, unfortunately," Elizabeth said. She kicked at a piece of fuzz on the carpet. "She said something about how I'm flinging myself into this too fast. And maybe she's right; I don't know. But being with Evan is the only thing that's kept me sane lately. So doesn't that mean it's the right thing to do?"

Tia was silent, and Elizabeth could hear one of her brothers yelling about something in the background.

"Tee? You told me the other day you understood."

"Well, yeah," Tia said. She didn't sound too certain.

5

"I mean, I get that Evan's helped you a lot lately. And I know he's a great guy."

"But?" Elizabeth prompted.

"Look, all I know is what happened to me after Angel left for Stanford. I was a total wreck. So when Trent came along, I convinced myself I was really into him. And he is cool and everything, but it was a serious rebound situation. And it ended up being a total disaster."

"But it's not the same," Elizabeth started to argue.

"Listen, Liz, I know this is important, but I really have to go," Tia cut her off. "Can we talk about this after the game?"

"Yeah, sure," Elizabeth said. "Oh, and good luck or whatever."

Tia laughed. "I'll pass that on to the team. Bye."

Elizabeth clicked off the phone, still holding it tightly in her hand.

So, Tia and Jessica both thought that her getting together with Evan was a bad idea. Along with the little voice in the back of her head, that made three of them.

Jessica pasted a huge smile on her face and ran out onto the field with the other cheerleaders. The weather was perfect—a sunny, crisp fall day. The smell of hot dogs and mustard gave the warm air that distinctive, game-day scent. But this was no ordinary football game—this was the big one: the last homecoming game of her high-school career. The crowd was on its feet, the players were pounding one another's shoulder pads and screaming into one another's faces, and Jessica was . . . just not into it.

Usually she fed off this group excitement—she loved being at the center of all the action. But right now she couldn't stop thinking about last night. And *not* about Elizabeth and Evan, although her self-centered sister seemed to think she was the only person who existed.

"Jessica!" Gina Cho hissed, jerking her head impatiently. All the other cheerleaders were standing two feet in front of Jessica in a perfectly spaced line. She scrambled into place and raised her arms over her head—just as everyone else lowered theirs in unison.

She heard an exaggerated sigh from her right and glanced over. Jade stood with her hands on her hips, shaking her head at Jessica as if she had just messed up a major move during the actual game.

Jessica scowled. Here was exactly the reminder she *didn't* need of what was bugging her so much. The last thing she wanted was to have to look at Jade's smug, condescending expression. Not after watching her dance with every guy in sight last night—clearly breaking Jeremy's heart in the process. And all Jessica could hear were her own words in her head, when she'd urged Jeremy to try to work things out with Jade. Because it obviously meant a lot to him, and maybe she was finally getting the whole putting-someone-else's-happiness-first thing. Maybe.

But Jade had already ruined her homecoming dance for her—she couldn't let her ruin the game too. She was going to have to pull herself together and concentrate on the cheers.

"Okay, everyone," Tia announced with a short clap. "Let's get started."

They got into position for their opening cheer in front of the bleachers. At least this was one Jessica could get through with her eyes closed. How many times had she done this stupid cheer anyway? Hundreds? Her body took over, and she mechanically performed the sequence of moves, even though she still couldn't push the image of Jeremy out of her head.

If Jeremy wants to be with Jade, a real friend would help him out, she told herself. She'd done the right thing. He had never been less than a good friend to her. Okay, he'd been a lot more than a friend. He was probably the most caring, romantic, funny person Jessica had ever known. And she had pushed him away. . . .

She finished the cheer listlessly and trudged back over to the bench, kicking the dirt with each step. Ahead of her, Jade walked with an extra bounce. *She* looked happy. No wonder Jeremy wanted to be with her.

"Are you okay, Jess?" She felt a hand on her shoulder and turned to see Tia standing there. Tia's long, dark hair was pulled back into a sleek ponytail, and she even had a little bit of makeup on—some lip gloss and mascara. Everyone here was psyched for this game—everyone except for Jessica.

Jessica sighed. "Yeah, I'm fine. Why?" she asked, avoiding her friend's gaze.

Tia gave a half shrug. "You just seemed a little out of it on that cheer."

"Just tired from last night, I guess," Jessica muttered, tugging at a stray strand of wool on her sweater sleeve.

Jade turned around. "We were all at the dance, Jessica," she said, rolling her eyes. "But you don't see anyone else forgetting where to stand. Luckily you can't get fired from cheerleading as easily as you can from HOJ."

"Jessica did fine," Tia snapped. "Get in position, everybody," she continued in a louder voice. "Time for the school song."

Jessica felt her shoulders sag in relief. She didn't have the energy to exchange obnoxious cuts with Jade right now. Along with the rest of the cheerleaders, she placed her hands on her hips and waited as the band launched into the SVH fight song. The crowd usually ignored this part, talking to one another right up until the game actually got started. But today the home-coming fans who had packed every corner of the

9

bleachers were on their feet, clapping and singing along. *Push everything else out of your mind*, Jessica thought. *This is supposed to be fun, remember?*

At least Jade was having fun. Jessica watched her out of the corner of her eye, watched how she made even the most routine moves look exciting, as if she was flirting with the whole stadium at once. *She probably is.* After all, when had having a boyfriend ever stopped Jade from turning down a date?

Jessica gave her head a shake and reminded herself to smile up at the stands as she completed the cheer. But she couldn't get the raw anger out of her system, and as she landed hard on her right foot, her heel caught in the grass and she stumbled forward. She thrust her arms in front of her to regain her balance just as the rest of the team's arms went straight up as they leaped into the air.

Great. Now it looks like I forgot the step, she thought. The game was just beginning, and she was already wrecking everything. People had said that senior-year homecoming was an experience she'd remember for the rest of her life.

It looked like they were going to be right.

"*Oof!*" Ken managed to mumble as he felt a sharp pain in his spine. He was lying at the bottom of a pileup, and an opposing player had driven his knee hard into Ken's back. Ken gritted his teeth to keep from crying out, but when the pile of struggling bodies on top of him cleared, he hopped up, making sure to flash a grin.

It was a good sign that the jerk had done that, actually—when the opposing team resorted to cheap shots, it meant they were getting frustrated. And Ken had them on the ropes now. He could feel it.

He glanced at the sidelines to see the referee moving the chains, signifying a first down. Ken felt several slaps on the back from his teammates. He chuckled as he jogged back to the huddle. The first play in the entire half when all of his receivers had been covered—and he'd scrambled for a sixteen-yard gain. That had to be a backbreaker for the defense.

He glanced around the circle of muddy faces, waiting for him to call the next play. It would be the perfect time to go deep, he realized. After that run the corners would be playing tight to contain.

"Let's go for it all," he said. "Todd, run a post. On three." His teammates nodded, then they broke and set up in the I formation. Ken could hear the crowd yelling, although the noise sounded like a muffled roar through his sweaty helmet. There was an electricity in the air, a feeling he hadn't had since last year. Mixed in with the homecoming signs were a bunch of signs saying, Welcome Back, Ken! This was his first big game since taking the position back from Will Simmons, and he was proving wrong anyone who'd had doubts about him.

He glanced at the sidelines and saw the cheerleaders

waving their pom-poms in the air. They'd been leading the crowd in special cheers for him. A high, clear voice rang out above the general clamor, calling his name. It was Melissa. He caught her eye, and she waved at him, beaming. It felt so great to have someone out there believing in him, supporting him. And she really did look cute in that cheerleading uniform.

Ken bent over the center to receive the snap. The center hiked him the ball on the third count, and Ken faked a handoff, then dropped back to pass. He glanced quickly at Todd. Single coverage—perfect.

He pumped once, faking a throw to the tight end. The cornerback fell for the fake and took a step toward the tight end, and Todd was by him. The cornerback had no hope of catching Todd, who was streaking toward the goalpost at full speed.

Ken felt time slow down as he reared back and lofted a high spiral downfield. The ball rose and rose, and for a moment it seemed to hang in the air, framed against the perfect blue sky. Meanwhile Todd was a full three steps ahead of his man, sprinting to get under the ball as it dropped from the sky. He caught it without breaking stride at the ten-yard line and jogged into the end zone, where he stopped and lifted both arms over his head.

Loud as it had been before, the noise in the stadium instantly seemed to triple. It was as if the air itself were tearing, shaking, the sound blending with the pounding on his back from his teammates. Forty-five yards in the air, and he'd led his man perfectly. You didn't see passes like that very often, even in college ball. There was no doubt about it. He was on, totally on. It felt like he could do anything.

Ken jogged to the sideline as Coach Riley sent out the kicking team for the extra point. The stands were a sea of ecstatic faces, and everyone seemed to be yelling his name. As he passed the cheerleaders, he slowed, waiting to catch Melissa's eye. She looked up when he was almost in front of her and gave him a huge smile.

Ken stopped, grinning back at her. Then suddenly Melissa stepped forward and threw her arms around his neck, squeezing her body against his. "You were amazing," she said into his chest. "Congratulations." Then she quickly let go and slipped back into line with the other cheerleaders.

Ken floated the rest of the way to the bench in a daze. It was overwhelming—the feeling of absolute freedom and power. He couldn't remember the last time he'd felt this good.

To: marsden1@swiftnet.com
From: mslater@swiftnet.com
Subject: Article

Hey, Andy—

I just had a great idea. Why don't you write an article about the Outdoors Club for the *Oracle*? We really need a change of pace—if I read one more feature on the football team, I'm going to throw up. And I know you'd be great at it—just write like you talk. It will be a perfect thing for your college applications. You could call yourself a "columnist" or something. And you'd be doing me a big favor. Please, please, please?

                                        Maria

Instant Messages

ev-man@swiftnet.com
Hey, Liz. I saw you were online too, and I figured as long as we're both not doing anything, why not do it together? Want to hang out?

lizw@cal.rr.com
[in private chat room]
Maria—I really need to talk. Are you free?

mslater@swiftnet.com
Sure. Come on over.

lizw@cal.rr.com
[back in public chat area]
Evan, sorry—I'm just heading over to Maria's. Rain check?

CHAPTER 2
Comforting Isolation

Will Simmons felt his blood drain to his feet as he watched Melissa pull away from Ken Matthews. From *hugging* Ken Matthews.

"Let's go," he blurted out to his mom, suddenly afraid he was going to be sick. He pressed his hands down on either side of him, pushing his fingers against the cold seat of the bleachers.

"Now?" she said with a frown. "But it's only half-time. And you haven't even said hello to Mel—"

Will clenched his teeth, forcing himself not to glance back down at midfield. He was dying to take another peek, to see what happened next with Melissa and Ken. But he knew if he turned his head one inch, his mom would follow his gaze to see what had upset him. And that could not happen. If there was one thing worse than total humiliation in front of the whole school, it was his *mom* trying to comfort him.

"I don't feel too good," Will mumbled, kicking at a huge plastic cup near his left foot. He kicked it again and was rewarded with a splattering of brown liquid on his jeans.

17

"Is it your leg?" his mom asked. He'd grown so used to that note of concern in her voice that he'd almost forgotten how it sounded when she *wasn't* worried about him. "Do you need to lie down and elevate it?"

Will nodded. "Yeah," he said. "I guess I'd better do that. But at home—not here." He struggled to keep his voice even. Here he was, making his first public appearance since his injury, and what did he find? Instead of missing him, the whole school seemed to have completely forgotten about him. There were signs everywhere saying, Welcome Back, Ken! And he couldn't help noticing that the crowd was behind Ken in a way they never had been with Will. It was like they were *glad* that Will was gone and their old quarterback had returned.

And Melissa . . . she was the reason he'd shown up here today. He'd actually felt guilty about pushing her away, so he'd decided to come to the game and support his girlfriend, even though it meant watching another guy do his job on the field. But she obviously couldn't care less about him. She was as happy to see Ken out there as everyone else was.

He grimaced as his mom helped him to his feet and handed him his crutches. This wasn't his school. He didn't belong here. All he wanted was to get back to the comforting isolation of his own room.

His jaw tightened as he made the effort to hobble forward on his crutches. It was pathetic—*he* was pathetic. This was why he hadn't wanted Melissa to see him. Not yet. Not until he could make it two steps without feeling like he'd just run a marathon. He stopped and clutched the railing, feeling his mom hovering right behind him, waiting to reach out and help if he needed it. Maybe for once he should let her. The sooner he got out of here, the better.

"Ken! Get over here!"

Ken's head jerked up at the sound of Coach Riley's gruff voice. He hopped to his feet and jogged to the far end of the bench, his helmet dangling by the face guard from his left hand. The band was just finishing its halftime program, so he was prepping himself for the second half of the game.

Coach Riley didn't even look up when Ken reached him. "Someone to see you. You've got five minutes," he said, his eyes never leaving the diagrams on his clipboard.

Ken glanced around, confused.

"Good to see you, Ken."

He turned, and right behind him stood Hank Krubowski, the University of Michigan scout. He recognized him instantly—the tall, broad frame under a blue-and-gold windbreaker, the thinning hair and narrow eyes. He'd first met the scout when he was a junior—then recently he'd seen him talking to Will about a scholarship. Before the accident, of course.

"I don't know if you remember, but my name is Hank Krubowski," he said, holding out his hand. "I'm with the University of Michigan athletics department."

"Yeah, I remember," Ken blurted out, shaking his hand. Every muscle in his body tensed as he realized what was happening. Hank Krubowski was scouting *him.*

He hasn't said that yet, Ken told himself. But what else could this be about?

"I know you've got a game to finish," Mr. Krubowski continued. "I just wanted to say hello and to make an appointment for next week."

"An appointment?" Ken echoed. He probably sounded like an idiot. But it didn't matter—the guy wasn't interested in Ken for his brain.

Mr. Krubowski laughed. "I'd like to ask you some questions about your plans for next year."

Yes. He had it—he was set. The football scholarship that he and his dad had dreamed of for years was actually happening. Just weeks ago he'd had to watch Hank Krubowski take Will Simmons out to celebrate *his* scholarship while Ken sat on the bench, and now . . .

"Ken? Does that sound okay?"

"Oh, yeah, of course," Ken said quickly. He licked his lips. "So, when?"

"How's Tuesday at five?"

Ken nodded, hoping he'd remember that. His

body was so filled with raw excitement right now that he didn't trust himself with important information.

"Great, I'll see you then." Mr. Krubowski turned to go, then looked back over his shoulder. "By the way, nice first half," he said. He strode off, seemingly oblivious to the fact that every guy on the team was watching him go.

Ken dropped down onto the bench, ignoring his teammates' curious stares. A month ago he had been worried about getting into a state school—and now he had a chance to play for one of the top-ten college teams in the country.

He picked up a ball lying on the grass in front of him and began spinning it in his hands. Hank Krubowski would be watching him in the second half. He really couldn't blow this now.

"Hey," a soft voice said, interrupting his thoughts.

He glanced up, surprised. Melissa stood in front of him, her hands clasped. "I saw you talking to Hank Krubowski," she said. "What did he want?"

"Oh, he—," Ken started, ready to blurt out the news to someone who'd be as excited as he was. But he cut himself off, realizing that Melissa might not be too psyched. He had this chance only because of what had happened to *her* boyfriend. A flash of guilt hit him as he thought about it. When he'd watched Hank Krubowski with Will, he'd wished it could be him instead. More than wished. It wasn't his fault that Will had gotten hurt, but it still felt weird knowing that everything he had now was thanks to someone else taking a bad fall.

"Um, he wants to see me," Ken finished. "Next week." He kicked at the dirt with his cleats, hoping she wouldn't lose it.

"You mean about a scholarship?" she asked. It was hard to tell from her voice exactly *how* she was reacting.

"Maybe," he admitted, a smile forming despite himself.

"That's great! Congratulations!" she said. Then, to his amazement, she leaned down and hugged him, like she had at the beginning of halftime.

Ken took in a short breath, unsure how to respond. It was great that she was able to be so happy for him, but wasn't it a little weird that she wasn't upset for Will?

What is my problem? Melissa was being a good friend, exactly what he needed. He was just used to Maria, someone who would never have been able to admire him for catching the eye of a Michigan scout. He let his arms close around Melissa, his hands brushing against the back of her soft red-and-white cheerleading sweater.

The horn sounded, signaling the end of halftime. Melissa stepped back, blinking up at him. The wind blew a wisp of hair in her eyes, and he felt a sudden, strange impulse to reach out and brush it aside, but she tucked it back behind her ear.

It was amazing how comfortable he felt with Melissa already, even though he still barely knew her. But they seemed to understand each other. With Maria, things were . . . complicated. But with Melissa, it was just easy somehow. Natural. Melissa knew what he was all about—and she *liked* him that way.

It felt good to be doing something he was good at again. Something he loved. And it felt great being around people who got why he loved the game.

He pulled on his helmet and fastened his chin strap. It was time to show Hank Krubowski what he could do.

Elizabeth pressed the Slaters' doorbell button for the third time, listening to the sound reverberate inside the house. She shifted impatiently, tugging at the bottom of the red SVH sweatshirt she'd thrown on before driving over. She felt like she couldn't stand still—like if she stopped moving, she'd have to *think,* which was very low on her priority list right now.

Finally she heard footsteps pounding closer inside, and then the door swung open.

"Hey, sorry," Maria said, slightly out of breath. Even with no makeup, Maria looked as gorgeous as ever. Her skin was smooth, and there wasn't even a hint of puffiness under her eyes. Elizabeth was certain that her own face could serve as the "opposite" photo of Maria's right now.

"Come on in," Maria said, leading Elizabeth into the living room.

They settled next to each other on the brown leather couch. Maria tucked her long, lean legs underneath her, then cocked her head at Elizabeth.

"So, what's up?" she asked. "Why aren't you at the game?"

"I couldn't deal with it today," Elizabeth replied.

Maria frowned in confusion. "*You* couldn't deal with it? Your jerk ex-boyfriend isn't even the star quarterback."

Elizabeth winced as she remembered seeing Ken at the homecoming dance last night with Melissa Fox. She wondered if she should tell Maria before she heard it from someone else.

"It's fine," Maria said quickly, obviously misunderstanding Elizabeth's reaction. "I'm just trying not to think about the whole thing." She stopped, pointing at a stack of videos sitting by the VCR across from them. "I camped out here last night with a bunch of movies," she explained.

"Any left?" Elizabeth asked.

Maria laughed. "Nothing you'd want to watch, unless you like movies about girls and horses. It was relive-my-childhood night. Hey, do you want some tea or something? I was just in the middle of making some when you got here. That's why it took me so long to answer the door."

"Yeah, tea sounds good," Elizabeth agreed. Maria jumped up, and Elizabeth followed her into the kitchen.

Maria turned the stove back on, reheating the teakettle sitting on top. Then she sat down across from Elizabeth at the round kitchen table.

"So, wait—you never explained why you couldn't handle going to the game," Maria said.

Elizabeth propped her chin on her hands and stared out the window over the sink. A squirrel was hanging upside down in order to raid the Slaters' bird feeder.

"I kissed Evan," she blurted out.

"What?"

Elizabeth turned back to meet her friend's gaze, seeing the shock in Maria's dark eyes. "Last night I kissed him. Actually, he kissed me. But I kissed him back."

"Well, you don't sound too happy about it," Maria said.

"I don't know," Elizabeth muttered. She grabbed the wooden saltshaker, spinning it around in her hands. "It just kind of . . . happened. At the dance." She paused. "In front of the entire school."

Maria's eyebrows shot up. "You're going exhibitionist on me now?" she teased.

Elizabeth groaned. "I know; it's crazy. But being

with Evan is the one thing that makes me feel good. Everything with Conner has been so hard, so *insane*. Then I see Evan, and it's all easy. It's like a time-out from the rest, you know?"

Maria shrugged. "Nothing wrong with that," she said.

"I know. But Jessica and Tia seem to think it's not a good idea. Going out with Evan, I mean."

The teakettle started to whistle, and Maria got up to pour two mugs full of hot water. "Which one do you want?" she asked. "Lemon Zinger or Mellow Mint?"

"I don't think I could handle anything with the word *zinger* in it right now," Elizabeth said.

Maria returned with two steaming cups of liquid, and Elizabeth took a sip, then held the mug at arm's length. "It's not working," she joked. "I'm still not mellow."

Maria laughed.

"Seriously," Elizabeth said, "tell me the truth. Do you think I'm totally nuts for kissing Evan?"

"I don't know." Maria stirred her tea with a spoon. "How do *you* feel about it? That's what matters."

Elizabeth took a breath, feeling like she was inhaling through a too-thin straw. "I just don't know. Freaked out, I guess," she admitted.

Maria's eyebrows furrowed. "Hmmm," she said.

"But now, every time I think of that kiss . . ." She took another deep breath, then tried to relax her shoulders, which were hunched practically up to her ears. "It's like the one calm thing in my life just became my biggest source of tension. What was I thinking?"

Maria took a sip of tea, then gently placed the mug back on the table. "Well, what *were* you?" she asked.

"Aren't *you* supposed to be telling *me?*" Elizabeth moaned.

"Why?"

"So I can tell you to mind your own business," Elizabeth said. "Instead of sitting here wondering if I just totally screwed up."

They sat there in silence for a moment. Elizabeth glanced back out the window, watching a pair of cardinals picking at the seeds the squirrel had kicked onto the ground.

"Maybe guys are just more trouble than they're worth," Maria finally said.

"Yeah." Elizabeth gave her a weak smile. "We used to hang out a lot more before Conner. Didn't it seem like things were so much easier last year?"

Maria nodded. "So let's do it," she announced. "Let's go do something completely mindless and silly, like we used to. Just us, no guys."

Elizabeth started to smile. "Like what?" she asked.

"Like . . . bowling," Maria declared.

"Bowling? Are you serious?"

"So we'll suck," Maria said. "So what?"

Elizabeth giggled. "You're right. I think *that* kind of pain would be a step up."

"We could invite Andy," Maria added. She cracked a smile. "Don't tell him I said this—but he doesn't really count as a guy, you know?"

"Well, we're in no danger of getting our hearts trampled by him, at least," Elizabeth said with a shrug.

"Okay, so I'm going to run upstairs and get changed. Why don't you call Andy?"

Elizabeth nodded, and Maria took one more drink of tea, then dashed upstairs. Elizabeth leaned back in her chair, staring down at her cup. Hopefully spending the day with her friends would distract her enough to let her brain figure out what she really wanted with Evan.

Jessica stood under the stream of hot water in the locker-room shower, relieved to finally be alone. She closed her eyes and held her face directly under the pounding spray, trying to let the rush of water wash away the past three hours.

She'd never messed up so many cheers in her life. By the time the game ended, she'd felt like crawling under the bleachers and hiding under a mound of hot-dog wrappers. It wasn't like she'd never tripped before, but to land flat on her face like that . . . She squeezed her eyes shut tighter, trying to blot out the memory, but the hot water stinging her scraped knees made it hard to forget.

She lingered in the shower until she heard the chatter in the locker room wind all the way down. When the last locker door had clanged shut, she yanked the shower handle hard to the left.

With the beating of the water suddenly gone, complete silence settled on the locker room, broken only by a slow, steady drip from the faucet. At last the muscles in her shoulders unclenched, and the air eased out of her chest in a long sigh.

She rubbed a towel quickly through her hair, then wrapped it around herself and walked into the bathroom. She stepped toward the mirror—then froze.

Jade Wu stood in front of the sink, leaning toward the mirror as she carefully applied mascara to her long, black lashes. Jessica's first impulse was to shrink back into the shower. But it was clear from the smirk that appeared in Jade's reflection that she'd already noticed her, so she continued into the room.

Jessica gritted her teeth, waiting for Jade to start in on her. She'd been on her case all day. Jessica was ready to run to the nearest pay phone and call Jeremy to take back everything she'd said last night.

Jade leaned back toward the mirror, slowly stroking the mascara brush up and down. She seemed to be enjoying Jessica's discomfort too much to spoil it by speaking. Jessica yanked a comb through her hair, then plugged in her blow-dryer, eager to hide behind the loud noise.

"Good game," Jade said casually. She stuck the mascara wand back in the slim bottle, then tossed it into her purse.

Jessica flinched. Was she making fun of Jessica's performance? Or just talking about the team's victory? "Yep," she grunted, then flipped on the dryer.

"Jess!" Jade shouted. Jessica looked back at her without turning off the blower. "Turn that off! I want to ask you something."

Jessica pressed her lips together, then flipped the switch and set the blow-dryer down on the ledge of the sink.

"What do you think: this"—Jade gripped the zipper at the bottom of her gray knit minidress—"or this?" She yanked the zipper, opening a slit up the side. Considering the clingy dress barely reached her thighs as it was, creating the slit was way over the top.

"It doesn't make any difference unless you're going to a job interview," Jessica said. She blinked. How clueless could she get? Did Jade really need to be reminded that Jessica had gotten her fired from HOJ?

Jade's eyes narrowed. "Thanks for your concern," she said. "But it's for a date." She stared straight into Jessica's eyes. "With Jeremy."

Jessica struggled to keep her expression blank, although there was a painful tug inside her.

"So which do you think Jeremy would like better?" she taunted.

"Why ask me?" Jessica said, reaching for the blow-dryer. "Judging by the number of people you danced with last night, coming on to guys seems to be your specialty."

Jade pulled a tube of lipstick out of her purse. "Jealous much?" she asked.

Jessica's grip on the hair dryer tightened. "Jealous?" she burst out. "How can I be jealous of thirty guys at once?"

"Well, Jeremy's not just any guy, is he?" Jade pressed. She leaned forward and applied her lipstick in two quick strokes.

No, he's not. He's the most amazing, incredible—

"I thought guys were all the same to you," Jessica said, trying to ignore her thoughts. "In fact, I didn't think you knew the word had a singular form." She was clenching the hair dryer so hard, she was afraid the plastic would crack.

For a second Jade's cool expression actually faltered. Jessica felt a pang of guilt. Maybe she had gone too far. She knew what it felt like to be called a slut. She bit her lip. "I just meant—," she began.

But before she could finish, she heard footsteps.

"Jade?" Coach Laufeld's voice echoed through the concrete corridors. "Jade, are you in here?"

"Yeah. Over here, at the sink," Jade called out.

Coach Laufeld stuck her head in the door. She was breathing hard. "Jade, I'm really glad I caught you. I just got a phone call. It's about your mother."

Jade froze, and her face paled instantly. "What?" she said. "What about my mother?"

"I'm sure she'll be all right," Coach Laufeld said quickly. "Apparently she, uh, passed out at work. She's in the hospital, but she's okay, really. Everybody's been trying to find you."

"Passed out? What do you mean, passed out?" Jade asked. Jessica had never seen her like this—she looked terrified. It was like the second their coach had mentioned her mother, she went into some different mode.

"I'm sorry," Coach Laufeld said with a shrug. She rubbed her forehead, looking very tired. "That's all I know. But I think you should go to the hospital right away."

"Yeah, I will," Jade said, her voice low and unsteady. She gathered the rest of her makeup from the sink and threw it all into her purse.

Coach Laufeld waited a moment, then seemed to realize there wasn't much more for her to say, so she turned and walked back out.

Jessica cleared her throat. "Do you, um, need a ride?" she offered. "Maybe you shouldn't drive right now." She wasn't sure, but it looked like Jade's hands were shaking.

"Don't do me any favors," Jade snapped, some of the color returning to her face. "I'm fine."

"Oookay," Jessica said, stepping backward. Here was the Jade she knew and couldn't stand.

"Just stay out of this," Jade said, then rushed out of the room.

"Happy to," Jessica mumbled to herself. But somehow she couldn't stop thinking about the way Jade had looked a minute ago. The girl was seriously freaked out about her mom. Maybe she knew something more than Coach Laufeld did. What if Ms. Wu was really sick?

"It's none of my business," Jessica told herself, finally switching the blow-dryer back on. There was absolutely no reason she should care anymore about Jade Wu.

HANK KRUBOWSKI

<u>Sweet</u> <u>Valley</u> <u>High</u>
<u>Homecoming-Game</u> <u>Notes</u>

The Matthews kid looked even better today. At least as good as last year's scouting reports. No sign the layoff affected his game. Just have to find out exactly why he was missing from the beginning of the season. Injury that could come back in the future? Make sure to check into it before meeting on Tuesday.

CHAPTER

3 Too Easy

Melissa stood in front of the guys' locker-room door, pretending to listen as Cherie Reese babbled about the football team's amazing victory. The parking lot was still full a half hour after the game ended, and people were hanging out by their cars, enjoying the sunshine and greeting the players as they emerged from the side door of the locker room.

"Forty-eight to fourteen! Can you believe it?" Cherie went on. "Ken was awesome today, wasn't he?"

Melissa shrugged. "The team played a great game," she said. The locker-room door opened, and two more players came out, but she didn't see Ken. "But yeah, Ken was definitely the star."

A silver BMW drove past, horn blaring, then pulled to a stop. The front window rolled down. "Hey," Seth Hiller greeted them. "You want a ride, Cherie?" he asked, giving Melissa a brief glare. He'd been really obnoxious to her at the dance last night when he saw her with Ken. Was he still on this whole defend-Will's-honor ride? As if Will even cared what she did.

"Go ahead," Melissa told Cherie. She'd been looking for a way to get rid of her friend so she'd be alone when Ken finally emerged from the locker room.

"What about you?" Cherie asked, giving her auburn hair a flip—probably for Seth's benefit.

"I'm leaving soon," Melissa lied. "I'll call you later. Really—go with Seth."

Cherie shrugged and pranced around to the passenger side of Seth's car, hopping in next to him. The door slammed, and they roared off. Melissa stared after them, frowning. It was good that Cherie and Gina and the others still felt like they needed Melissa's okay on things. But she was worried about what would happen if Seth and Will's other friends kept up this stupid act with her.

Soon enough, Ken will be so popular that those guys won't matter around here anyway, she reassured herself.

Just then Melissa heard a round of cheers coming from behind her. She turned to face the locker-room door again and saw Ken heading out. His short, blond hair was damp from the shower, and his cotton shirt showed off his broad shoulders and lean chest. But she got only a quick glimpse before he was surrounded by people congratulating him, including a bunch of alumni who were psyched to see the guy who'd brought their old school some glory. And of course there was a bunch of girls gazing at him adoringly.

Melissa pulled her letter jacket tight around her. She wouldn't be part of the crowd. Not her style.

Soon enough, Ken—and the people around him—got closer. She could hear everyone yelling things at him at once.

"You were awesome, dude," a guy said.

"Yeah! You were *sooo* amazing!" a female voice piped in. Melissa cringed. How pathetic. Did she really think being a doormat was going to make him notice her?

"Where you headed, man?" asked another guy. "Want to get some pizza?"

"Yeah, a bunch of us are heading over to Guido's. You coming?"

Then Melissa heard Ken's deep voice. "I'm not sure," he said.

As they got closer to her, Melissa was careful to keep her gaze focused on the parking lot, as if she were waiting for someone else. Ken could never think she was actually here for him.

"Hey, Melissa," she heard him call out just when the crowd was right next to her.

She held back a satisfied smile, then turned to look at him.

"Oh. Hi, Ken," she said calmly, as if the two of them were alone.

"So, uh, Melissa. You feel like getting some pizza?" he asked. Everyone else got quiet, listening. Ken had asked her in front of his many admirers, which was definite points for her. Now all she had to do was get him away from that crowd.

She shrugged. "Thanks. I'm not really hungry, though."

Ken stuck his hands in his pockets. "So what about just going for a ride?" He glanced around him awkwardly. The girls were starting to walk away, obviously getting the message. "We could go to the beach or something."

"Um, I did have other plans," Melissa said, staring back at the parking lot as if watching for her phantom ride home. "But it was nothing important." She smiled at him, pretending to ignore all the eyes on her. "Sure, let's go," she agreed.

"So, I guess I'll catch you guys later," Ken said, turning to the people who still stood around him.

This had been too easy.

"Your turn, Liz," Maria called.

Elizabeth looked up as Maria returned to her seat. There were still seven pins standing. Maria wasn't smiling.

Elizabeth set down her paper basket of cold french fries and wiped her greasy fingers on her jeans. Maybe bowling hadn't been such a good idea. She'd forgotten how long you had to wait between turns. A game with such long pauses was not the best way to take your mind off things—most of the time there was nothing to do *but* think. As soon as her turn was over, she'd go right back to worrying about Evan. She hadn't even noticed Maria take her turn.

"All right! There they go," Andy said as the machine swept the pins away. "A spare for Maria."

"I think you're only supposed to count the ones I actually knock down, Andy," Maria said.

Andy picked up his pencil. They'd gone to the one bowling alley left in the world that hadn't switched over to computerized score keeping yet. "There's no time limit," he pointed out. "The pins are down now, right?"

"Whatever." Maria slumped into her seat, her arms hanging over the armrests.

Andy set the pencil back down. "You're supposed to argue," he said.

"Why?" Maria asked, sounding as drained as Elizabeth felt. "It's just a stupid number on a piece of paper we're gonna throw away in half an hour anyway."

Elizabeth set her ball back on the rack and narrowed her eyes at Maria. She'd seemed fine this morning, but something had changed while they were at the bowling alley.

"Are you okay?" she asked. She walked over and plopped down next to her on the yellow plastic chair.

Maria sighed. "No," she admitted. She glanced back and forth between Andy and Elizabeth. "Look, I promised myself I wouldn't ask, but I have to. Was Ken at the dance last night?"

Elizabeth wiped her palms on her jeans again, even though they were dry. "Yes, he was," she said quietly.

"Did he . . . have a date?" Maria squeaked.

Elizabeth looked at Andy, who gave a helpless shrug. They had to tell her the truth. But Elizabeth knew how much this was going to hurt Maria.

She cleared her throat, but her tongue felt too dry to speak. "Um, Andy?" she said.

Andy sat forward, his hands on his knees. "Yeah, he went with someone," he said.

Maria nodded. "Okay," she said. "So, who?"

There was a long silence, filled only by the echo of rolling bowling balls and the crash of pins.

"Melissa Fox," Andy finally said.

Maria's eyes darted back to meet Elizabeth's. "Melissa?" she asked. The pain on her face made Elizabeth ache.

"I think it was probably just that with Will hurt, neither of them had a date," Elizabeth explained. "I'm sure it didn't mean anything."

Maria shook her head. "Oh, come on. You know how Melissa works. She's a quarterback's girlfriend all the way, and Will's not the quarterback now. I should have seen it coming."

"But it might not be anything like that," Andy said.

"Right." Maria didn't sound too convinced, and—unfortunately—Elizabeth wasn't either, despite what she'd said. Ken and Melissa had looked surprisingly cozy last night. They hadn't seemed like two friends at a dance together. It was more like . . . the way she and Evan had been.

But weren't we just supposed to be friends too? There was no way she could keep telling herself that.

"Okay, you know what?" Elizabeth said, standing up. "This bowling thing is *really* not working. We're all just getting more depressed. Personally, I'd much rather be eating a hot-fudge sundae."

"I'm in," Andy said. "Not here, though. They'd probably keep setting up another as soon as you downed the last one."

Maria gave a weak laugh.

"Sorry. It was a great idea, Maria," Elizabeth said.

"I like Elizabeth's better," Andy said. "I could definitely go for some ice cream and chocolate. That's supposed to be the best way to deal with a pathetic love life, right?"

"Thanks for reminding us, Andy," Maria said.

"Yeah, seriously," Elizabeth agreed. She didn't have to worry about being reminded, though. Because being reminded would mean she had managed to forget about it for more than thirty seconds. And the way this day was going, that would be cause for celebration.

*   *   *

"This is her room," the nurse told Jade, pointing to a door with the number 612 printed on a metal plate. "You can go in now."

"Thanks," Jade mumbled. She'd barely ever been to hospitals, and somehow she felt like she wasn't supposed to speak too loudly, like in a library. She stared at the door for a second, taking a deep breath, then pushed it open.

The lights were off, and the shades were drawn over the small window on the opposite wall. There were two beds in the room, but one was empty. Jade dragged her gaze to the other bed, her heart pounding hard.

Her mother was sleeping peacefully, the sheets pulled up over her. But one arm was on top of the blanket, and Jade could see the sleeve of the thin blue-and-white hospital gown. Her breath caught when she spotted the white plastic band around her mom's wrist—her hospital ID bracelet. Why was her mom wearing that? Why was she *here*?

Then she noticed the tube connected to her mom's arm, inside her elbow. Were they giving her some kind of medication?

Jade swallowed, then took a few steps closer to her mother. The wall behind her bed was filled with all kinds of equipment and monitors that Jade had never seen before.

"Mom?" Jade whispered.

Her mother's eyes fluttered open. "Jade," she said.

She smiled. "Thank goodness they found you. I hope you weren't too worried."

"Are you all right?" Jade asked.

"I feel fine," she responded. "They just want to watch me for a little while."

"Then what's that for?" Jade asked, pointing to the tube.

Her mother glanced down, flexing her arm. "They're giving me fluids," she explained. "It's nothing serious, I promise. I guess I just skipped a couple of meals without realizing it, so I was dehydrated. That's what the doctor said—exhaustion and dehydration."

Jade held her mother's gaze, trying to see if there was something she was holding back. But she seemed to be telling the truth. Jade let out a deep sigh.

"So all of this is just because . . . you missed dinner?" she asked, resting her hand on the metal rail on the side of the hospital bed.

Her mother closed her eyes and shook her head. For the first time Jade noticed how exhausted she looked—she could see the tiny creases on her face and the deep circles under her eyes.

"Jade," she said softly. She reached out and covered Jade's hand with her own. "There's something I have to tell you."

Jade gulped. She'd known there was something else going on, something big. God, she couldn't take it if her mom was really sick. She really didn't know what she'd do.

"You know how I've been out so late all the time lately?" Ms. Wu began. "And I've told you it was because I had a lot of dates?"

Jade nodded, confused. What kind of doctors had late night appointments? Specialists in some really bizarre disease?

Jade pulled her hand free and stared at her mother. "What are you trying to say?" she demanded. Whatever it was, she needed to know—now.

"I haven't been on dates," her mother admitted. "I have a second job, a night job. I'm a waitress at the Sidecar bar downtown. That's why I'm never home, and the doctor says it's why I ended up here. I've just been pushing myself a little too hard, he said." She paused, shaking her head. "Maybe he'd like to help me pay the rent, then," she muttered.

Jade clenched and unclenched her fists, trying to process everything her mom had just said. "So, there's nothing else wrong, then—with your health?" she asked. "You're really okay? Not sick?"

Ms. Wu smiled. "I'm really okay," she promised.

"Well, why didn't you tell me about your other job?" Jade asked. She sank down into the visitor's chair a couple of feet away. "I mean, I don't understand why you had to lie to me." She and her mom always told each other everything. At least, that's what she'd thought.

"I didn't want you to worry." Ms. Wu shook her

head again. "You know that our financial situation isn't very good. But things have been tighter than ever lately, and I took the second job a few months ago to help get you through your last year of high school."

Jade's heart sank as she imagined her mother holding a tray over her head as she worked her way through a crowd of drunk people, on her feet, after working an eight-hour day at the bank. And part of this was her fault too. A huge part. She was the one who kept getting fired from job after job. She'd really messed up big time.

Jade noticed beads of sweat forming on her mother's brow. Talking about this was obviously just making her more stressed.

"Mom, just relax, okay?" Jade pleaded. "Don't worry. I'll get another job soon, I promise. And we can cut down on stuff. The money isn't worth you getting sick."

Ms. Wu nodded. "Yes, I will have to cut down my hours at Sidecar. And we're going to have to economize a little more."

It killed Jade seeing the guilt in her mother's eyes. She felt like *she* was letting Jade down because she couldn't give her expensive stuff. Jade was the one who'd let her mom down.

"I have some really good job leads already," Jade lied. "I bet I'll have something definite by the end of this week."

She leaned over and kissed her mother's cheek, leaving a light mark from her lipstick. She couldn't help thinking how much her lipstick had cost—and her mascara, her shoes, her haircut, not to mention her dress, all bought with money her mom had earned carrying drinks around in the middle of the night. And all this time Jade had thought her mom was out partying!

She squeezed her mother's hand. "Everything will be all right. Just take it easy, okay?"

"I will. Sorry about dinner. There's some soup in the freezer," her mother said, sinking back onto her pillow. "They're holding me here for observation tonight, but I'll be home tomorrow."

"Hey, don't worry about me. I'll be fine," Jade said. "You just rest."

She watched until her mom's eyes closed, then tiptoed out of the room, gently shutting the door behind her.

Ken,

I guess it's been a long time since I left a note on the fridge. But it's been a long time since we had something to celebrate, right?

It's nice having a reason to be proud of you again. How about a victory barbecue?

—Dad

CHAPTER 4
Jessica Number Three

"Hello?" Jessica called out as she let the front door slam behind her. There weren't any cars in the driveway, but she still wanted to make sure she really had the house to herself. She dropped her cheerleading bag on the hallway floor. Her mom hated it when she left it there, but she was too worn out to drag the bag downstairs to the washing machine. Besides, she could do it later, before her parents got home.

She wandered into the kitchen and poured herself a tall glass of skim milk, then plucked the sheet of yellow lined paper dangling from the refrigerator magnet and sank into a chair to read the note. *Went shopping for patio furniture, then out to dinner. There's a roast in the fridge. Love, Mom.*

So that explained her parents, but what about Elizabeth? Jessica had expected to find her still moping around the house. She really hadn't been looking forward to another round of "should I be with Evan or shouldn't I?" It was so obvious that Elizabeth was just using him, and Jessica was sick of watching. She set her empty glass in the sink with a bang and then strolled out into the backyard.

What's wrong with this patio furniture? she wondered, picking at the frayed edge of the white polyester strap on one of the folding recliner chairs.

So far, this day was not going well. First a fight with Elizabeth, who was too obsessed with Evan and Conner to even think of asking how Jessica was doing. Then the worst cheering of her life and that whole weird thing with Jade in the locker room.

Jessica pulled a thread loose from the side of her chair. What difference did it make? They were getting new furniture anyway.

She frowned, her mind going back to Jade and the look on her face when she heard her mom was in the hospital. Jessica couldn't imagine what it would feel like to get news like that about her own mother. And at least she had her dad, and Steven, and even self-absorbed Elizabeth. Jade had no one but her mom.

If that were me, I'd be freaking out, Jessica thought. She had a sudden impulse to go call her and make sure everything was okay.

What's my problem? Jade hated her, and she hated Jade. Jessica was the last person in the world Jade would want to hear from right now. She'd made that very clear in the locker room.

But Jade could be home by herself right now,

really upset. She didn't have a lot of friends, and she wasn't the type to ask for help.

Maybe she should tell someone, someone who Jade wouldn't push away. But who? None of the other cheerleaders would be home yet. They'd all be out partying after the game.

Restless, she got up and walked back inside, standing right next to the patio door. Who would she want to talk to if her only family member were in the hospital?

She pressed her head against the window, the glass feeling cold and sticky against her forehead.

It was an easy answer. But could she really do that? Could she push the person who mattered most to her toward Jade *again*, even after the way Jade had treated her today?

Get over yourself. This was serious. The girl's mother was in the hospital. And he—for whatever reason—really cared about Jade. He'd want to know if she was in trouble.

Before she could change her mind, she went into the kitchen and picked up the phone, then dialed Jeremy's number.

Jeremy's eyes blinked open when he heard the phone ring. He stared at the TV in front of him. Instead of players passing a ball on the field, there was some woman out in a jungle. He must have fallen asleep before the game ended.

The phone rang again, and Trisha, his six-year-old sister, dashed across the living-room carpet and grabbed the receiver.

"Aames residence," she said. "Yes. He's here. Is this Jade?" Jeremy suddenly felt tired again. Then Trisha's face burst into a huge smile. "Oh! Hi, Jessica!"

Jeremy sat up, his heart pounding.

"Okay. I'll get him," Trisha said. She turned to Jeremy and held out the phone. "It's for you."

Jeremy crossed the room, wiping his sweaty hands on his pants. It was crazy the effect this girl had on him. Just knowing she was on the phone made him feel a million different things at once. And it didn't help to have to wonder which Jessica would be on the other end—the one who had seemed to be flirting with him last week or the one who'd spent last night pleading with him to work things out with Jade.

"Hello?" he said, taking the phone from Trisha. She didn't make a move to leave, and he waved his hand in a shooing motion, turning his back on her.

"Hi, Jeremy."

"What's up?" he asked.

"I'm actually calling about Jade." Her voice was eerily calm. Almost emotionless—something he could rarely say about Jessica. "I have some bad news."

Jeremy frowned. Apparently it was Jessica

number three—the one who'd dragged him down to the beach just to bust Jade with another guy.

"Look, if this is just gossip or rumors about Jade, I'm not interested," he said. Why did Jessica always have to play these games? If she wanted him, couldn't she just come out and say it?

There was a long silence, and for a second he thought she was going to hang up.

"Just listen a sec, Jeremy," she said in that same even voice. "This is important. Jade's mother is in the hospital."

"She's what?" he asked. "What happened?" Instantly Jeremy flashed back to the moment he'd heard those words about his father, when his dad had a heart attack. The fear he'd felt then was still so close to the surface.

"I don't know," Jessica stated. "Coach Laufeld said it was nothing serious, but Jade seemed pretty freaked out. I was in the locker room with her when she found out. She was going to the hospital straight from the game, so she's probably back home by now. I just thought you should know."

"Yeah, thanks," Jeremy said, staring at the receiver in shock. He'd been a jerk to think Jessica was pulling something. She had gone out of her way to let him know that Jade—someone she'd made it clear she couldn't stand—was in trouble. She was really amazing. More amazing than he'd ever given her credit for.

"You're right," he said. "I should probably go check on her." It was awful, but he really didn't want to hang up with Jessica. He wanted to let her know somehow that he was sorry. Sorry for not getting what a good friend she was, how she really had always been trying to help. Sorry for not admitting to her—or even to himself—that what he really wanted was more than a good friend.

Jade, he thought. *You're supposed to be thinking about Jade.*

"So, I guess I'd better get going," he said reluctantly.

"Yeah, I guess so," Jessica said. For the first time he could hear emotion in her voice—and he almost thought she was as sad to hang up as he was. "Bye," she said. The phone clicked off in his ear before he could say anything else.

Why did every conversation with Jessica seem to go like this? Just when he thought he had her figured out, she did something totally unexpected.

The only thing he *had* figured out for sure was that he and Jade didn't belong together. He'd decided that last night, even though Jessica kept telling him to make things work. But he knew all too well what Jade was going through right now, and he was going to be there for her. The rest could wait.

Melissa squeezed the soft leather of the passenger seat of Ken's Trooper as he accelerated around the curve. She snuck a look at the speedometer. He was going pretty fast, and the road was filled with tight curves. Should she say something?

Ken was bobbing his head up and down, immersed in the booming beat and wailing guitar from the stereo. The muscles in his forearms rippled as he spun the wheel sharply to the left. This time the car's back wheels actually skidded. She glanced at Ken. He was smiling.

He knows what he's doing. He was just still on that high from the game. She'd seen Will like this before. Well, not *quite* like this. Even when Will was psyched, he was always focused. Ken just seemed completely free. It was exciting to be around. It made her feel like she could share in that freedom somehow and not have to worry about Will, or their future, or anything else.

They whipped around another curve, and Melissa felt her heart jump. Maybe this was a little *too* much freedom.

"Ken?" she said. "Ken?" She put her hand on his shoulder, and he turned and grinned. "Can we slow down a little?" she shouted.

Ken's window was all the way down, and her hair flew all around her face.

"Don't worry. You look fine," he replied, missing the point. He took his right hand off the steering wheel and reached over, tousling her hair even more. He laughed, then put on a burst of speed and passed a low-slung silver sports car.

Melissa smiled weakly. She turned down the music. "Are you sure you don't want to tell me where we're going?" she asked. He'd promised her an interesting destination but hadn't said anything more. Another way he was totally unlike Will, who always needed to have things planned out and agreed on from the start.

"You'll see," he said, smoothing back his own hair.

"Well, how much longer?" she asked.

"It's right . . . here!" he said, suddenly lurching into the exit lane. He gripped the wheel tightly as they whipped down the exit ramp. He slowed down as they got off on a bumpy road, then screeched into a cracked parking lot covered in piles of drifting sand.

"I bet you didn't know there was a beach here, did you?" he asked, turning off the engine. The sudden absence of the radio's pounding sound made her sigh in relief.

"No," she said, wide-eyed. Since he was obviously into surprising her, she might as well play it up.

He sprang out of the car and came around to her side. Then he opened her door and extended his hand to help her out. When she was standing beside him, he took her other hand and looked into her eyes. "You know what?" he asked.

The sun was low in the sky behind him, forcing her to squint back at him. "What?" she asked. The wind was blowing the edges of her skirt up, and she wanted to smooth it down, but he was holding both her hands.

He leaned toward her, his eyes glowing with pride. "I think that was the best I've ever played in my life."

"It was pretty incredible to watch," she told him in her most admiring tone.

"I still can't believe it. It was like every single thing I tried worked. Everything. I wish I could tell you what that feels like." He grinned, looking almost sheepish, but she could see the excitement in his eyes. He shook his head, as if trying to release some of the energy built up inside him. "Come on," he said. He let go of her hands and headed for an opening in the dunes.

Melissa followed, feeling the sand scratch inside her expensive leather shoes. She followed Ken down a trail in the sand between two dunes anchored by salt grass and emerged on a narrow stretch of beach.

The sound of the surf, indistinguishable from traffic noise on the other side, was now a loud roar. It wasn't much of a beach, but they were the only ones on it, which did give the place a romantic feeling.

Ken beckoned her down to the shoreline, where the waves were surging up a shallow incline and receding back into the sea. "Isn't this great?" he asked. "I thought you'd like it. I come here when I want to get away." He paused, his eyes narrowing. "I know things haven't been easy for you, and even though I'm happy about playing again, I'm sorry that it's only because of what happened to you and Will."

Melissa smiled. Ken was the only person who got that Will's accident hadn't just "happened" to Will. Her life had been changed completely too. Even Will couldn't see that, but Ken did.

She strolled up to him slowly, feeling the wind cut through her thin shirt. She wished she hadn't left her cheerleading sweater back in Ken's car. She hugged herself as a chill shot through her.

"Cold?" Ken asked.

She shook her head and smiled.

"Yes, you are. I can tell. Come here."

She stepped toward him tentatively, and he wrapped his strong arms around her. She nestled into his chest, sheltered from the wind.

"Look," he said.

A wave was rushing toward them, and she reflexively tried to step back, but she was locked in his grip and couldn't move. She gasped as the water surged closer, slowing as it approached, until the wave died just inches from her shoes and sank into the sand. Ken laughed.

It had been a long time since she'd been with someone where she didn't feel in control. She knew how to make sure Ken wanted her, yeah, but she really never knew what he'd do next. There was something exciting about that feeling of mystery or anticipation.

"This has been a great day," she murmured. "Thanks for taking me here."

Ken stared out at the ocean. "I know what you mean," he said. "I wish I could just take this feeling and . . . I don't know." He closed his eyes and inhaled slowly.

"It seems like you've been getting better and better every game," she said. "Next week you'll probably throw six touchdowns." She gave him a squeeze, and he smiled. "I can't wait to hear what Hank Krubowski has to tell you," she said, ignoring the twinge of pain as she remembered sitting across from Hank at the brunch where he'd officially offered Will a scholarship. That was the past, and she had to leave it there if she wanted to get anywhere in the future.

"It really felt great out there today," Ken said. "And hearing you cheer for me helped. Really. Just knowing everyone was behind me made it so much easier." He turned to face her, his blue eyes intense and shining with happiness. His face was inches from hers. Her lips parted slightly, expectantly, and she could feel his warm breath on her cheek. The muscles in his face softened, and he started to lean toward her.

Then he blinked, and she could feel him draw back. *Too soon,* she thought. He wasn't ready yet for things between them to be more. But he would be soon.

"What's that sound?" she asked, furrowing her brow in concentration.

He cocked his head. "Just the wind, I think. Are you still cold?"

She nodded.

"Let's head back, then," he said.

She clasped her arms tightly around her chest as Ken guided her back to the parking lot, one hand protectively on her shoulder.

She smiled to herself. That gesture alone meant way more than a kiss. It showed that Ken already felt the need to take care of her. He was getting attached—she could feel it. And they were way ahead of schedule.

Evan Plummer

Okay. Time to meditate.
Clear your mind.
No thoughts.
<u>Ommm. Ommm. Ommm.</u>
No—stop thinking of Elizabeth.
<u>Ommm. Ommm.</u>
Just forget her for one minute, okay?
Just let it go. You're as
scatterbrained as Jessica.
<u>Ommm. Ommm.</u>
Focus.
Okay, forget it. You know you're going
to think about Elizabeth no matter what
you do. You might as well just enjoy it.
Elizabeth . . .
I wonder what she's thinking right
now?

CHAPTER

Glory Days

5

Melissa waved at Ken as his car raced off, kicking up a spray of loose gravel. So what if he hadn't kissed her good-bye? She wasn't worried. She could tell when a guy was into her, and it was obvious that Ken liked her. It wasn't hard to read the signals.

He was clearly the hot guy of the moment, the rising star in the social scene. And she'd been there, ready to snap him up before anyone else even knew what was happening.

She smoothed out her rumpled clothes and opened the front door. The TV in the living room was on—that was strange. Her parents barely ever watched TV, and if they did, they usually just watched the one in their room upstairs. She walked into the room, about to go turn off the TV, when her breath caught.

Will was sprawled out on the sofa, his crutches propped up against the coffee table. His eyes went right to her, narrowing into a sharp glare.

"Will!" she gasped. "What are you doing here?"

"Waiting for you," he said, a bitter edge to his

voice. He sat forward, running a hand through his gold-brown hair. "I was at the game today, but you didn't see me. I guess you were kind of busy."

Melissa bit her lip. "How long have you been here?" she asked.

"I don't know. About an hour and a half, I guess. Your dad let me in, but then he had to go out." He turned off the TV and set the remote control on the mahogany end table. "Where were you?" he asked. "The game ended three hours ago."

"I got something to eat," she lied, avoiding Will's gaze. She walked over and sat down at the other edge of the sofa, then started straightening the papers on the coffee table, trying to keep her hands busy while she wondered exactly how much Will knew. Had someone told him about her going to the dance with Ken last night?

"So, why didn't you tell me you were coming to the game?" she asked, turning the focus back on him. "I guess you're feeling better."

"Uh-huh," he said. She risked a quick glance at his expression, and she could see the muscles of his jaw clench and unclench.

"It was a great game," she said.

"I wouldn't know. I left at halftime." He paused, as if to let the words sink in. Then he cleared his throat. "Who'd you go out to eat with?"

"Why do you care?" she snapped. "What did you expect me to do? Go home and sit in the dark, waiting

64

for you to call? You haven't spoken to me in days. Now I'm not allowed to talk to anyone else either?"

He blinked a few times, but his body remained rigid. "Does that mean you're not going to tell me?" he asked, his voice cold. "Why not? Is there something you don't want me to know?"

She shoved aside the papers and crossed her arms over her chest. "What is this—some kind of test?"

Will snorted. Actually snorted. "You were with Matthews, weren't you?" he said.

"So what?" Melissa asked, her voice rising. "You wouldn't even answer your phone. Do you have any idea what it's been like for me? All I wanted was to be with you, but *you* pushed *me* away."

"Oh, so I *made* you go out with Ken?" He slammed his fist on the sofa. His whole body was trembling. She'd never seen him like this. He was out of control—out of *her* control.

"Which is worse, Will?" she demanded. "Me hanging out with a friend, someone who's been decent to me lately, or you refusing to speak to me? How do you think that made me feel?"

"You're always the victim, no matter what happens, aren't you?" Will shook his head. "My entire future goes down the tubes—my college scholarship, my football career—everything. *Everything*," he repeated, staring at his cast. "But I guess none of that compares to the pain of an unanswered phone call, does it?"

She followed his gaze, looking at the cast that covered his whole right leg. She flinched, then glanced away, back at the coffee table in front of her.

"Your life did not end just because you hurt your knee, Will," she argued. "You have a choice. If you want to just give up and throw everything away, I can't stop you. But you can't expect me to throw my life away too."

"What's that supposed to mean? Now that I'm not the quarterback, being my girlfriend means throwing your life away? Man!" His fist slammed into the cushion again. "I just needed some time alone. I never dreamed after all we've been through—after all the times I've been there for you—that you would ditch me the second I got hurt." His eyes were gleaming with anger so intense, it scared her.

"What do you call breaking up with me when I was in the hospital so you could be with Jessica?" Melissa countered. "How dare you accuse me of anything after that?"

"Five years," he said quietly. "Five years of always, always being there for you. And just *once* I need you for a change, and that's too much to ask." He shook his head slowly, his eyes never leaving hers. "Maybe I had it right the first time. Maybe we should have stayed broken up."

Melissa felt dizzy. A part of her wanted to lunge toward him, cling to him, cry, apologize, anything to stop where this was going. But she couldn't move a muscle.

A car horn honked, and she jumped.

"That's my mom," Will said. "I called her to come pick me up." He struggled to his feet, obviously in pain. She let her eyes linger on him and realized how much weight he'd lost and how pale he'd gotten.

"So I guess that's it," Will said, watching her. "It's over."

Don't go. I love you, Will.

Why couldn't she just say it? Even after the way he'd treated her and seeing him so weak, she needed him. He was part of her after all these years, and she couldn't be near him without hurting.

But he was a wreck, and she couldn't let that happen to her. He was an angry, bitter wreck.

Will turned away when she didn't say anything, then hobbled to the front door. She winced as she heard it slam behind him.

As soon as she knew he was gone, her shoulders sagged. What was she doing? This was *Will*—her rock, her future, her life. Was she really going to let him walk away?

Just then the phone rang. It took a second for her to register what the noise meant—the shrill, piercing sound. She sat on the edge of the sofa, the ringing drifting in and out of her awareness. Then she heard the roar of an engine outside. Will and his mom pulling away.

She glanced over at the source of the screeching in her ear—the cordless phone resting on the coffee table. With a sigh she grabbed it.

"Hello?" she said.

"Hey, Melissa?"

It sounded like Ken. The band around her chest loosened, and she could breathe.

"Yeah, it's me," she responded.

"It's Ken. Did you finally, um, warm up?"

She sank back against the sofa cushions. "Yeah, I guess," she said.

"Good." He paused. "So, I had fun today."

"Yeah, I did too," she said, keeping her tone light.

"I was wondering if you were free tomorrow, actually," he continued. "Like, for dinner?"

Breathe. Breathe.

"Sure," she said. "I'd love to."

"Cool. See you tomorrow. I'll pick you up at six," he said.

She smiled, even though he couldn't see it. "Great. See you then."

When she hung up the phone, the pressure in her chest started to return. Ken's voice faded, and all she could think of was Will's worn, pale face.

But she wasn't doing anything wrong. Will had walked out on her, not the other way around. What was she supposed to do? She'd tried to be there for him, but he wouldn't let her.

And this time she wasn't going to get pulled

under. She'd been there before, and it was an ugly place. She'd vowed never to let that happen again. So she'd do whatever it took to keep that promise.

You come home to an empty apartment every night, Jade told herself as she closed the door behind her. *You've been alone here lots of times.*

But this time was different.

All those other nights she knew her mom would come home eventually. Ms. Wu was supposed to come home tomorrow morning, but what if something changed? What if she had to stay in the hospital for longer?

Jade dragged herself into the kitchen, suddenly aware of how tired she was. That nerve-racking time in the hospital was more draining than a month of cheerleading stunts. It was like weeks had passed since the game this morning. It seemed so silly to remember how pumped she had been for homecoming—the game, the dance. As if those things really mattered.

She tugged open the freezer and took out a container of frozen soup, then plopped it in the microwave. It was still hard to believe: All those nights her mother hadn't been out partying; she'd been working a second job. How could she not have noticed?

She drummed her fingers on the microwave. When had her mother even made this soup? She shook her head. She was going to drive herself crazy if she kept this up.

But the questions wouldn't stop. Her mom was only cutting back her hours a little now. But if she got worse, the night job was history. If they'd been tight for money before, what then? Would they have to move to a smaller apartment?

The microwave dinged, and Jade took out the soup and scooped several spoonfuls into her mouth directly out of the plastic container. It was time to face facts. High school was almost over. In a few more months she'd be on her own anyhow. She just had to grow up a little early.

Tomorrow she'd go out first thing and look for a job. Restaurants were open on Sundays. But there was nothing she could do now.

She went into the living room and switched on the TV. Usually she was so beat after a game that she could zone out instantly. But tonight the words all ran together, and she couldn't concentrate.

The doorbell rang, and she jumped. She had no idea who would be here, but the idea of company was such a huge relief right now. She ran out into the hallway and pulled open the door, forgetting to even ask who it was first.

She broke into a wide grin when she saw who stood in front of the door.

"Jeremy!" she said, throwing her arms around his neck.

"Hey—are you all right?"

Jade shook her head and pressed her face against Jeremy's broad chest. At least when she had been alone, there had been a surreal distance to everything—a numbness. But now that someone else was there, she couldn't just turn on the TV and try to forget about it. The whole thing suddenly seemed inescapably, unavoidably real.

"I can't believe this is happening," she murmured. "One day you have a normal life, and the next day your mom is in the hospital."

"What happened?" he asked, softly stroking her back. "How's she doing?"

Jade pulled back slightly. "She collapsed at work," she explained. "They say it's just exhaustion and dehydration, and she's coming home tomorrow, but it really freaked me out. Nothing like this has ever happened to her before."

She was faintly aware that her makeup was all smudged and faded, but for once she really didn't care that Jeremy was seeing her like this. She was just so happy he was here.

"Hey, come in," she said, stepping back so he could walk by.

He followed her back into the living room, and she switched off the television.

"I know how scary it is to see someone you love in the hospital," Jeremy said, sitting down next to her on the sofa.

Jade nodded. "This isn't that serious," she said. "At least, that's what my mom told me. But I also found out she's been working this other job I didn't even know about, and she's still barely able to pay all our bills. And my dad isn't exactly a huge help."

Jeremy closed his eyes for a second, leaning back his head.

"What is it?" she asked.

He looked at her, his gaze intense. "It's just I know what you're going through," he said. "I never told you what happened with my dad this year. He had some serious heart trouble and lost his job. We almost had to sell the house. For a while there I was working double shifts at HOJ to keep food in the kitchen."

"Wow," Jade said. "I had no idea."

"Everything is fine now—he has a great job and everything," Jeremy added. "And I'm sure things will be okay for you and your mom too."

"I hope so," Jade said. She picked up the green throw pillow and started flipping it around in her hands. "But I have to get a job, like, tomorrow. And I can't mess up again like last time." She pulled her feet up onto the couch in front of her, hugging the pillow to her chest.

Jeremy put his arm around her, and she laid her head on his shoulder. He stroked her back silently.

"Why are you being so nice to me?" she asked softly, snuggling her head closer to his neck. "I mean, after the way I treated you last night." She might not have admitted it to Jessica, but she knew she'd been a jerk to Jeremy. She'd just been so afraid to let him know she actually cared about him after the way he'd brushed off the "anniversary" date she'd thought would be so important for them.

"Hey, forget about last night," he said, resting his hand on her shoulder. "It's not even an issue."

She turned her head to look up at his face. "But I totally ignored you. Weren't you mad?"

"It doesn't matter, okay?" Jeremy said. "I'm here now, right?"

"Yeah, you are." Why had she needed to see some kind of silly proof that he cared? He was here when she needed him. Obviously she meant something to him. It was time to let herself trust that.

"You know, I only wanted to make you jealous," she admitted. "Because—because of how I feel about you," she almost whispered.

He shifted, pulling her head tighter against his chest. She couldn't see his expression, but she could tell everything she needed to know from the way he held her. She'd never said anything like that to a guy before—let him know that she felt something. But Jeremy wasn't going anywhere.

She pulled her head back again. "I must look like a mess," she blurted out. She could feel her bangs sticking to her damp forehead.

"You look great," Jeremy said. "That's one thing

you never have to worry about. You always look great."

Jade laughed. "Now I really can't believe anything you say," she teased. "But thanks." She nestled into his arms and tilted up her head to kiss him lightly on the lips. The sensation of being so close to him was almost enough to erase all the fear and anxiety swirling around inside her.

"Are you going to be okay tonight?" he asked. "I actually have to get home to baby-sit my sisters, but you can come with me if you want—if you don't want to be alone."

She smiled. Jeremy was as thoughtful as ever. But as much as she loved Trisha and Emma, she wasn't sure she could handle all their energy tonight. "Thanks, but I'm okay," she replied. "I'm just glad you came."

His dark eyes grew serious. "Your mom is going to be all right," he promised. "And anything I can do to help, just let me know."

She nodded. "I will."

He gave her a kiss on the forehead, then stood up, stuffing his hands in the pockets of his khaki pants. "Listen, um, I've got this banquet thing on Tuesday night," he blurted out. "It's a dinner for the Big Mesa honors students. They give out awards and stuff. Do you want to come? It won't be superexciting or anything, but—"

"No, it sounds great," Jade interrupted, grinning.

He wanted her to be his date at a major event. School functions weren't high on her list of fun things to do, but still—everything was more fun with Jeremy. And the important part was that he really *did* want them to be a couple.

"Cool," he said. "Well, I'd better get back home."

She walked him out to the front door.

"Remember," he began, his hand on the door-knob, "if it gets lonely around here, you can always call me. Don't worry if it's late—I've got a phone in my room."

"Thanks. And thanks again for coming over. I was kind of freaking out."

"Everything will be better tomorrow," Jeremy said. "Right now part of it is just the shock. It's really scary to see a parent sick."

"I feel better already." She gave him one last hug. "Go home—go," she teased, pretending to shove him toward the door.

How could I be so lucky? she wondered after he'd left. She'd treated him like dirt, but he hadn't let her push him away. As soon as he'd heard she was in trouble, he'd ...

Jade stopped, frowning. How had Jeremy known to come over? From the second she opened the door, he was asking if she was okay. But she'd been too upset to wonder how he knew that her mom was sick.

The only people who knew were Coach Laufeld and ... Jessica.

Jessica had seemed genuinely worried about Jade in the locker room. She must have called Jeremy. But why would Jessica do something like that if she was so dead set on keeping them apart?

Jessica had to have known that she would send Jeremy right over there if she told him. The girl wasn't stupid. Was it somehow possible that Jessica knew exactly what Jade needed and . . . cared?

"Five touchdowns. I'd say that calls for a beer." Mr. Matthews plucked a can of beer from the dwindling six-pack in the cooler and tossed it to Ken.

Ken caught the damp, slippery can and popped the top. This was the biggest compliment in his dad's vocabulary—it was his way of showing Ken he was an equal. The only other two times he'd given Ken beers were when the SVH team won state and when he was named league MVP.

"Tell me again what Krubowski said—his exact words," Mr. Matthews said, wiping a hairy forearm across his forehead, which was dripping with sweat from leaning over the glowing coals in the barbecue. "Remember, I talk to these guys all the time. You can tell a lot from the little things."

"Just what I told you. I don't remember exactly," Ken said. For some reason, it kind of bugged him how obsessed his dad was with hearing every detail. He tipped back the foaming beer and swallowed a large mouthful.

"Michigan." His father pronounced the word with the same reverence some people would use for schools like Harvard or Yale. He stuck a long-handled fork into one of the two monstrous steaks on the grill and lifted one side to examine the bottom, then lowered it to cook a little longer. The smell of singed beef filled the backyard with a rich, satisfying scent that reminded Ken of the Fourth of July.

"They don't fool around in the Big Ten," Mr. Matthews said. "You'll be playing against future pros, you know."

"Yep," Ken said.

"You've got a real shot here, you know that?"

Ken didn't answer. He stood watching his father buzz around the patio, cooking his victory dinner, feeling nothing. After all, this was the same guy who had completely ignored him for months. But now Ken had thrown a few touchdown passes, and all of a sudden they were supposed to be best buds again. They'd come to an understanding, but Ken still couldn't forget his anger entirely.

His father put some paper plates on the plastic patio table and set a knife and fork on each one to keep the wind from blowing them away. He transferred the blackened steaks to a platter and set it on the table. "This is like old times, isn't it?" he said.

"What do you mean?" Ken asked.

Mr. Matthews frowned. "Just—like before."

You mean, before you practically disowned me

because I wasn't playing football, Ken thought. He sat down and cut into his steak.

"Good, huh?" his father prompted. Ken nodded, unwilling to give him the satisfaction of a reply.

Mr. Matthews studied him thoughtfully. "I know it's been a tough few months. But you came through." He paused. "And it's good to have you back," he said.

I didn't go anywhere, Ken thought. *I've been here all along. Where were you?*

But there was no point in going into it. What his dad thought didn't matter anymore.

They ate in silence for a few minutes, and as memories of that afternoon's game kept popping into his head, he couldn't help feeling good, especially as he relived his fifty-yard fling to end the first half. He'd been fantasizing about that play with every toss since he was about six, and now he'd done it.

"That last pass before halftime?" his dad said, as if reading his mind. "Man." He shook his head in admiration, and Ken grinned in spite of himself. "And right after you took that big hit too. Believe me, scouts notice that stuff. I've read enough of their notes to know what they look for. The first play after a big hit says a lot." He laughed out loud. "You showed Krubowski." He leaned back and crossed his hands behind his neck.

Ken chuckled. "Those guys were pretty frustrated. They were going for my eyes by the end of the game."

"That's when you know you got 'em beat," his father said with a grin. "Here." He slid another beer across the table.

Ken took a long drink and felt the warm glow spreading outward from his stomach. He'd felt so on top of his game today, moving the team downfield for score after score. He'd felt unstoppable, and for one day, he had been. To do that with Krubowski watching was a dream come true.

"You know what's funny?" he said, slamming the can back on the table a little harder than he'd meant to. "The trash they were talking before the game. 'You're going down, Matthews, just like Simmons.' 'I hope you got a good doctor, Matthews. You're gonna need one.' Those jerks got what they deserved."

His father shoved a huge bite of steak in his mouth. "I remember one game," he said while chewing. "I was down, and someone tried to kick me in the face. I grabbed his foot and twisted. Kid was out two weeks." He wiped his mouth with a paper towel and took another bite, glancing at Ken with an almost *shy* expression. Like he was looking for something from his son.

Then it hit him. He'd always looked up to his father as bigger, stronger than him, the ultimate jock he'd never live up to. But today he'd not only lived up to his father's career—he'd outdone him.

The feeling was disorienting, and he wished he didn't have a can of beer in his stomach. He found himself looking at his father like he'd never seen him before, like he was just some balding, middle-aged guy—still strong but way past his glory days.

As his father continued to prattle on about the teams to watch in the Big Ten, Ken felt like he was watching the whole conversation from a distance. When it came right down to it, how well did he know his father? All they talked about was sports. He'd gotten much closer to Maria in a few weeks than he had to his father in seventeen years.

Maria. Why was her name popping into his head? For a while this fall he'd felt like she was the only one who got him. But now that he was back on top again, it seemed like she was the one person who *didn't* understand him.

She'd really been there for him when he was at rock bottom. More than anyone else—more than his father, that was for sure. But what kind of person only wanted to be around you when you're hurting? His dad might not have known how to deal with him, but at least he didn't have a problem with Ken being happy again.

His dad finished telling some story Ken had heard a hundred times, but Ken smiled, and his dad smiled back. Maybe they understood each other more than he'd thought.

melissa Fox

Last night I dreamed I was in my living room, watching the Rose Bowl on TV. The camera went down the line of cheerleaders, and suddenly I saw myself, wearing a michigan uniform. The camera zoomed in for a close-up, and I looked really happy.

Then suddenly I was down on the field, cheering. The michigan quarterback threw a long pass, and it went for a touchdown. As everyone else was celebrating, he ran straight toward me with his arms out, like he was going to give me a hug. But when he got to midfield, all of a sudden he collapsed in pain, clutching his leg.

The whole crowd stood up and started booing and pointing at me. The cheerleaders were all yelling at me too. They all crowded around me until I started to panic.

Then everybody else disappeared—the team, the crowd, the cheerleaders, everybody—and I was standing in an empty stadium, alone.

Jeremy Aames

Okay, I'm a wuss. I know it. But as soon as I saw Jade looking so vulnerable and scared, there was nothing else I could do. I've been there—only I had my mom and my sisters. She doesn't have anyone.

It's probably even worse to stay with her just because I feel bad, knowing that I'll have to break up with her someday. But it's not in me to kick a person when she's down.

I just know that this can't end well.

CHAPTER
Total-Jerk Territory

6

Nothing's going to be there, Elizabeth told herself as she stared at the pile of yesterday's mail sitting on the table in the foyer. Every day since Conner had left for rehab, she'd had this crazy idea that he'd write to her, but he hadn't—of course. And why should he? They were over.

She hung her jacket up in the hall closet and went upstairs to her room. She turned on the computer, waiting for it to run through the start-up so she could open her e-mail. Andy had said he wanted help with the article he was doing for the *Oracle,* so she figured he might have sent her a draft.

I wonder if they can send e-mail from rehab? she thought.

But she didn't have any new messages—not even one from Andy. Then she remembered that he had said he might want to talk things over with her before sending her a draft. Before turning off her computer, she noticed an e-mail Evan had sent last night. She chewed her lip as she read the quick note again. It really wasn't fair to avoid him like this. If she was in his place, she'd expect to at least be able to talk to the person she'd kissed the other night.

The only problem was, she had no idea what to say.

Maybe it would be better to wait a little longer until she got things sorted out. As far as Evan knew, she'd had plans with Maria yesterday. He couldn't be offended by that.

The phone rang, and she reached for it with relief, figuring it was Andy, calling about his article. The *Oracle* was the one familiar constant left from her old, stable life.

"Hello?" she said, sliding into her armchair and draping her feet over one side.

"Hi."

She sat up straight.

"It's Evan."

"I know." Her heart thumped inside her chest.

"So, did you have a good time with Maria yesterday?"

"Yeah, um, we went bowling."

"That's cool."

There was a brief silence. It was weird not to be talking. But what was she supposed to say? *About that kiss—bad idea?*

Elizabeth stood up and began pacing the room. This obviously wasn't going to work. Talking to Evan was supposed to make her feel better, not worse. She had to do something.

"Listen," she said. "I think . . . I think . . ."

All at once it felt like there was an immense distance between her and everyone else in the world. Her room was too big; no one was home; Conner was miles away.

And here was someone who really cared about her. And she was about to cut him loose?

"Are you okay?" His voice was soft, impossibly gentle.

No, I'm not, she wanted to scream.

But it's not fair to keep leading him on, she thought. *I can't dump all this on him.* But all she wanted at that moment was to feel Evan holding her, comforting her, and telling her everything would be okay.

"Liz?" The tenderness in his voice made her press her lips together until it hurt. "Do you want me to come over?"

She squeezed her eyes shut and covered the mouthpiece with her hand, trying to get her emotions under control. "I'm okay," she said. "I think I just need some time alone."

"Are you sure?" he said. "Maybe I could help. I'd really like to see you," he added. For the first time she could hear a hint in his voice of what had happened between them at the homecoming dance.

"I really need to be by myself for a while," she said. "I—I was just thinking about Conner," she blurted out. His name seemed like the one thing that could serve as a wedge to put some distance between them right now.

"Oh." He was quiet, in that awful way. She hated it. "Hey, I totally understand," he continued. "No pressure."

"Thanks," she said. "Well, I'd better go."

"Okay." There was a long pause. "If you need me, call, okay?"

Elizabeth nodded, then realized he couldn't see her. "Yeah, I will," she said, then hung up the phone. She flopped facedown on her bed and pulled a pillow over her head.

Everything was just too messed up. Until she was ready to make a decision and stick to it, she shouldn't even talk to him. She hadn't realized what a total basket case she was, but hearing Evan's voice had just seemed to make her fall apart.

From now on she wouldn't pick up the phone without letting the answering machine screen it first. Next time she spoke to Evan, she'd give him a clear answer.

All she had to do now was figure out what it would be.

Jeremy slammed his history book shut and pushed back his chair. This was ridiculous. He'd read the same chapter four times, and he still couldn't say what it was about.

All he could think about was Jade and what he'd

gotten himself into. Was it right to pretend he was there for her when in his heart he knew he wasn't interested? To go through the motions just felt wrong, no matter what the reason was. He was only setting her up for a bigger fall later. But what else could he do? He couldn't abandon her, not now.

He stood up and went to the closet, changing into an old T-shirt and some shorts. He grabbed his running shoes from next to his bed and slipped them on. Running a few miles would clear his head or at least make him less stressed out.

He jogged down the stairs and out the back door to stretch out in the driveway. With one hand against the garage to steady himself, he grabbed his right foot and pulled it up and back to stretch his quadriceps. He did the same with his left foot, then sat on the pavement and reached for his left foot, bending over as far as he could.

Who was he kidding? There was nothing worse than extending a doomed relationship. He was going to have to tell her the truth. He grabbed his other foot and leaned over. It wasn't like he couldn't still be there for her. He'd be more there, really, because he'd be there for real. As a friend. Jade might not like it at first, but he could prove he really did care about her and still wanted to spend time with her. He could help her through this a lot more by being a real friend than a fake boyfriend.

He stood up, shook out each limb, and was about

to take off when his father came out of the house in a tan polo shirt and tennis shorts. Jeremy stared at him in puzzlement.

"Where are you going, Dad?" he asked. "You're not playing tennis, are you?" His father was a lot better, but it wasn't that long ago that he'd been flat on his back, looking pale as a sheet. Tennis seemed like pushing it.

His father laughed. "No. Just going for a walk. It looked like a nice day to be outside. Where are you off to?"

"Going running." His father did look pretty healthy. He was even showing some color against his light summer clothing. "Nice tan, Dad."

His father got a basketball out of the garage and hoisted one from the free-throw line. It bounced off the rim of the hoop they had in their driveway, and Jeremy chased it down the sidewalk. He bounced the ball to his father. "Best out of ten?" he suggested.

"You're on," Mr. Aames said, then dribbled over for a layup. "Good news," he said over his shoulder as he jogged over to retrieve the ball. "We landed a really big client this week. Signed yesterday."

"That's great!" Jeremy said. His father's broad, easy smile was so full of confidence, it amazed him. It wasn't that long since Jeremy had been scrounging dinner for his sisters from boxes of macaroni and cheese. Now his father was co-owner of a promising Internet start-up.

"Yep. Business is good. We're on track for a June IPO." He approached Jeremy, holding the ball in the crook of his arm. "I don't know if I ever told you how proud I am of the way you handled yourself this fall. Your mother says you were a real rock around here while I was sick."

Jeremy shrugged. "It wasn't that big a deal," he said. He grabbed the ball away and took a shot, making the basket easily.

He didn't want his dad to know what a nightmare that fall had really been for him. Always broke, always worried about his father's health and whether they'd lose the house—there hadn't been one stress-free moment in a day.

And that's what Jade's facing now, he thought.

"I don't know how you kept your grades up through all that," Mr. Aames commented, wiping some sweat from his forehead. "And now you're even getting an award at that banquet too. I'm so sorry that your mother and I have to go to my office party that night. I wish I could be there for you."

The awards banquet. He'd promised to take Jade. He couldn't break up with her before that.

"You know, son, nothing tells more about a person than how he comes through in the clutch, when you really need him," his dad said, reaching up his arms for a pass.

Like Jade needed him now. Jeremy glanced away, feeling the guilt eating at him.

Whether he and Jade had a future together didn't matter. What mattered was helping Jade get through this rough spot. Then he could deal with whatever came next.

Ken drove slowly up the tree-lined street, admiring all the immaculate lawns and huge houses. Until he'd dropped Melissa off yesterday, he'd never been in this section of El Carro.

It was amazing how fast his life had changed. A few weeks ago his football career seemed over—and he was going out with Maria. Now he was suddenly a big star again—and he was picking up a girl he barely knew.

It's not like we're dating, he thought as he rounded the corner and pulled up in front of Melissa's house. He and Melissa were just hanging out. She still had a boyfriend.

Maybe. It seemed like she and Will were on their way to splitting up. The guy wouldn't even *talk* to her. He was being a jerk, even if he was dealing with a lot.

Before he'd turned off the engine, the front door opened and Melissa came out, wearing a velvety shirt and an extremely short skirt that drew his eyes right to her slender, perfectly shaped legs. She waved and headed over to his car.

I wonder why she doesn't want me to knock? Maria was always so into him meeting her parents. But

Melissa *wasn't* Maria. And that was a good thing.

He opened the passenger-side door of his Trooper as she approached, and she climbed in, tugging her skirt down her thighs.

"Hey, what's up?" he said.

She frowned, looking down at her hands. She wore a silver band around one of her small, thin fingers, and her nails were a pale pink. She looked back up at him. "Will and I broke up," she said.

"Oh—I'm sorry," he said, squinting. It was obvious she was hurting, but her voice was clear and solid. Like if she'd just told him about a test for history instead of announcing that she and her long-term boyfriend were over. He shifted uncomfortably. The engine made the little catching sound it always did when the car was idle for too long, and he lightly touched his foot to the accelerator, giving it some juice.

"It was the only choice," Melissa said. "I mean, he wanted me to be as depressed and bitter as he is, and that's not going to happen. Plus he was mad about—" She paused, meeting Ken's eye. "About us," she finished. "He saw me hug you at the game yesterday, and he knew I went for that drive with you afterward."

Ken swallowed. He really didn't want to be the *reason* this supercouple broke up. Okay, maybe dinner tonight *was* kind of a date. Maybe that was borderline slimy on his part since he knew about her and Will. But he still didn't want to cross the line into total-jerk territory.

"But it's not about you," Melissa added, as if sensing his thoughts. "Will can't respect me, and I'm not going to take that." She inched closer to him. "Let's just forget about Will, okay? Let's go have a great time, like we always do together. Wherever you want to go."

She was right—they did always have fun around each other. Like at the beach yesterday. For some reason, instead of picturing him and Melissa at the beach, he thought about the time he'd taken Maria there. *That* had been a great night.

He shook his head, then leaned over and turned on the CD player, filling the car with the loud beat. That would get his mind off Maria. He took off down the street, then rolled down the window and rested his elbow on the door, feeling the breeze. This was more like it. Maria would have been complaining about the noise by now, but Melissa wasn't. And he didn't have to talk if he didn't feel like it. No cross-examinations.

A nagging thought in the back of his head kept bugging him. Was that really what he wanted— someone he didn't have to talk to?

He stopped for a red light and glanced over at Melissa. "You sure you're okay?" he asked.

She nodded, beaming up at him. "I'm great," she said. "Now that I'm with you."

She seemed to really mean it too. It was pretty amazing that he could do that for her. Melissa didn't expect anything of him. She admired him for exactly who he was, and just being with him made her happy. It was all so easy. So right.

He glanced up at the light. Still red. On an impulse he leaned over and pressed his lips against hers. She responded, softly at first. Then she wrapped her arms around his neck and moved closer to him, kissing him back—hard. And all his other thoughts and doubts just floated right out of his mind.

To: mslater@swiftnet.com
       lizw@cal.rr.com
From: marsden1@swiftnet.com
Subject: *Oracle* article

Hey, girls!

Here's a first draft of my article on the Outdoors Club. Be gentle.

Did you ever feel like something was missing? Like there was more to life than sitting around the house, playing *Tomb Raider* for twelve hours at a stretch? That just maybe there was some higher goal, some loftier purpose to aspire to?

Me neither.

That is, until I met with Mr. Nelson, our school guidance counselor. Not only did he tell me something was missing from my life, but he told me what it was: extracurricular activities.

Until that day I had found my regular-curricular activities to be more than sufficient, possibly even a little excessive. It had certainly never occurred to me to ask for any extra ones. But Mr. Nelson explained that with no extracurricular activities, my college applications ran the risk of appearing two-dimensional.

I don't know about yours, but my college applications are all on flat pieces of paper, so I didn't see the problem with this. But apparently despite their flatness, it is important for your college applications to appear "well-rounded." As we all know, being well-rounded requires that all-important third dimension. This is how I ended up joining the Outdoors Club.

Why the Outdoors Club? you ask. For one thing, it turns out almost every other extracurricular activity requires some sort of actual talent or skill, like playing a musical instrument, mastering a sport, speaking a language, or knowing how to play chess. It didn't seem likely that any of these clubs was looking for rank beginners with the skill level of a thirteen-month-old poodle.

The Outdoors Club, on the other hand, seemed to require only that you go outdoors. I go in and out of doors every day, I thought. How hard could this be? So I joined.

Hold on to your seat for this part.

It turns out that what members of the Outdoors Club like to do is climb up big, steep things called mountains. Personally, it seems to me that falling off a mountain is the kind of thing that could turn you from a three-dimensional being into a two-dimensional shape, which would seem to defeat the purpose of doing extracurricular activities in the first place.

This is where the ropes come in. Anticipating the danger of falling a long distance and ending up very, very flat, perhaps even two-dimensional, the members of the Outdoors Club developed the strategy of tying themselves to things. That way if they fall off a mountain, instead of landing with a splat, they dangle in the air, flopping like a fish until someone reels them back in so they can give it another go.

Having climbed mountains of homework in my regular-curricular activities, I felt prepared to try doing it with a real mountain. It was hard at first, but soon it became fun. You get to work hard, breathe fresh air, and look at the world from a whole new angle (especially if you rope up wrong and end up dangling upside down, as happened recently to a certain new member of the group who shall go nameless out of respect for his relatives).

That's pretty much all I have to say about the Outdoors Club except for this: The Outdoors Club is a great place to practice conquering your fears. Have a fear of being tied up? Lots of practice, guaranteed. Fear of falling? Fear of heights? Come on down. Fear of looking ridiculous? We provide the opportunity—the rest is up to you. But believe me, opportunities galore are there for the taking.

After just a few weeks in the Outdoors Club, I found that conquering my fears became sort of a habit. Certain things I'd been avoiding for years were transformed from terrifying obstacles to challenges I was no longer so afraid to tackle. Would I have faced them otherwise? It's hard to say. But I'm glad I did. So even if the Outdoors Club does not get me into the college of my choice, I'm still glad I joined. I don't know what more you could ask from an extracurricular activity than that. Except possibly a little patch for my jacket.

CHAPTER 7
Karmic Thing

It's just school, Elizabeth told herself as she walked through the front doors of Sweet Valley High on Monday morning. She wasn't used to being scared to come here. But she'd managed to spend the rest of the weekend hiding out in her room, avoiding the phone. And now that option was gone. As she walked down the hallway, she couldn't help feeling like everyone was staring at her. *There's the girl who made out with her date in the middle of the dance Friday night.*

What other people think isn't the problem. Sometime today she was going to run into Evan, the one who *did* matter. And she had no idea what to tell him—still.

She rounded the corner to her locker and stopped short. There he was already. Waiting right in front of her locker. Her first impulse was to back away, but then he looked up, and their eyes met. It took all her concentration just to keep her feet moving with some kind of coordination, and then she reached his side.

Her one hope all weekend had been that seeing him would give her a gut reaction that would help her know what to do. But all she felt was panic. Unless that *was* the gut reaction she should be listening to.

"Hi," she said. She pressed her sweating hands against her thighs, feeling the rough fabric of her jeans.

Evan cocked his head to one side, causing a loose lock of long, black hair to fall across his forehead. His hands remained casually shoved in the pockets of his khaki cargo shorts. "How's it going?" he asked.

All he has to do is put his arms around me, and I'm going to start crying, she thought. But standing here frozen in indecision was even worse.

"Are you okay?" Evan asked.

Why did he have to *care* about her so much? If he needed too *much* from her, it would be easier to step back and say she couldn't handle it. But he seemed fine—no sign of two sleepless nights like hers. All he seemed to care about were *her* feelings—which unfortunately were the last thing in the world she wanted to discuss.

The traffic in the hall was picking up—it was almost time to go to class. Evan reached out slowly and ran his fingers through her hair. She leaned her head against his hand. It felt so good just to let him be there for her. Maybe she'd been thinking too much. Why *shouldn't* she be with Evan? What had she been so afraid of?

Listen to yourself, she thought. *Aren't you forget-ting how freaked out you were about that kiss Friday?* She blinked, trying to clear her head. If she didn't get out of here fast, she was going to be in even deeper. The last thing she needed was another kiss to worry about.

As if on cue, the bell rang. She stepped back, avoiding his gaze.

"I'd better get to class," she mumbled. Feeling like an idiot, she turned and fled.

"Nice look, Jessica. Very New York."

Jessica snapped out of her reverie in time to wave as Annie Whitman slid by down the hall. She glanced down at her black jeans and black crop top. Her choice of color had not been a fashion state-ment. It was just the way she felt today, as if she was in mourning for the remotest possibility of a normal love life.

You did the right thing, she told herself. *You did the right thing.* But no matter how many times Jessica repeated it, the thought was replaced seconds later by an image of Jeremy hugging Jade. And if she failed to erase the image in time, Jeremy would look at her over Jade's shoulder with this sad expression, as if to say, *This is all your fault.*

On Saturday it had seemed so noble to push Jeremy back toward Jade. Now it seemed totally crazy. How did she know what would make him happy? Why had she interfered? Jeremy probably wasn't even anything special to Jade—just one of twenty dance partners on a Friday night.

Noble sacrifice was one thing. Pointless sacrifice was another.

Someone jostled her as the crowds trickled into classrooms. She couldn't stand out in the hall forever. But Jade was in her next class. She could at least wait until the second bell.

"Jessica?"

Jade. Not a voice she wanted to hear right now. Jessica summoned all her self-control and turned to face her.

Jade's hair was damp, as if she'd just woken up in time to take a shower and throw on the slim-fitting tank dress she had on. She wasn't wearing any makeup, which normally wasn't an issue for her, but today her face was blotchy and red. Dark circles stood out under her eyes.

"Are you okay?" Jessica blurted out.

Jade cracked a smile. "I look that good?" she joked. There wasn't a trace of her usual attitude.

"You just look . . . tired," Jessica explained as they fell in step next to each other. Jessica pushed a few strands of blond hair back behind her ear. "How's your mom doing?" she asked.

"She's better," Jade said. "Thanks. Actually, that's kind of what I wanted to tell you. To thank you, I mean."

Jessica stopped, scrunching up her face in confusion. "For what?"

"For Saturday night. With Jeremy. It was really, um—it was nice of you."

It seemed pointless to pretend she didn't know what Jade was talking about, so she just nodded.

"I also wanted to apologize," Jade continued.

"Jade—"

"I know what you think of me," Jade interrupted. "And maybe I have been kind of a bitch lately. I just wanted to explain. I know this sounds stupid, but I really thought you were trying to break up me and Jeremy. But when you called him on Saturday—" She swallowed and looked down at her open-toed sandals.

"It's no big deal. I just thought he would want to know, that's all," Jessica mumbled. She could deal with an angry attack. But the last thing she was ready for was an apology—especially since until three days ago she *had* been trying to break them up.

"Anyway, thanks," Jade said.

"It's okay, really," Jessica said. They started walking again. Jessica hugged her books to her chest. "So, um, is your mom home yet?" she asked.

"Yeah. She has to take a couple of days off work, though. More rest." Jade's facial muscles tensed. Maybe Jade and her mom were in worse trouble with money than Jessica had realized.

And I'm the reason Jade got fired from HOJ. She cringed inside.

"My mom's health is okay, I think," Jade continued. "But I need to find a job, pronto."

"Yeah," Jessica said, feeling like the ultimate slug. But Jade had been pretty obnoxious to her, and she *hadn't* been a very good worker. Still, if Jessica had known that Jade needed the money that badly . . .

"Things with Jeremy are good, though," Jade added as they brushed by a big crowd of football players. "Thanks to you. I know I made a fool out of myself at the dance Friday, but he told me on Saturday that none of that matters. He even invited me to this academic-awards banquet at Big Mesa. Serious boredom city, right?"

Jessica forced out a weak laugh. It was the kind of conversation she and Jade would have had a long time ago, when they were friends.

"No, really, I'm psyched about it," Jade said. "Being with Jeremy is worth it."

"Great. That's really great," Jessica said. Where was the second bell? She needed an excuse to take off down the hall, rush to class, get away from these stories of how *happy* Jade and Jeremy were together.

"I have this black dress that I think would look perfect for it," Jade went on as they kept walking. "I just wish I still had that silver necklace, though. Remember that one I took off to clean the cappuccino machine, and it fell in the garbage disposal? It would have been great."

"Mmmm," Jessica replied, listening to the click of her heels against the floor.

Finally the second bell rang, and Jessica's head snapped up. "Oops—we'd better run," she said.

"Yeah, okay. But Jess—thanks again. Really. You're a good friend."

Friends? Was that what they were again? This was all too strange. But at least Jade's mom was okay. And she and Jeremy were back on track, which meant he'd be happy. That was what Jessica had wanted, right?

Yeah, right.

"Coming up next: parents who think their teens are growing up too fast. Right after this."

Depressing, Will thought. He changed the channel. Soap opera. Soap opera. Infomercial.

Will heard a knock on the door and hit the power button.

"Will?" his mother said, poking her head in his room. "I'm going to the store. I thought you might want to come."

"No, thanks," he said, glancing down at the sweats he'd been wearing since yesterday.

Mrs. Simmons hovered in his doorway, her eyes darting around his room. "It's a beautiful day," she said. "I thought a little exercise might do you good. The doctor said—"

"Sorry. I don't really feel like it."

She paused, running her hand along the door frame. "Have you thought any more about going to the physical-therapy session the doctor told you about? I think you'd feel better if you started moving around a little bit, don't you?"

What's the point? Why bust his butt at physical therapy and hurry back to school so everyone could watch him limp around like a cripple?

"Is the pain still bad?" his mother asked, her voice trembling slightly.

"Sometimes, yeah. Especially when I move," Will said.

"But the doctor said that if you walked around more—"

"It hurts, okay?" He glared at his mother. She looked away, biting her lip.

"Maybe next week," he said. What was the big rush to get back to school anyway? Without football the whole thing was just a hassle.

"Okay. Well, feel better. I'm off," she said. She didn't move, but he turned the TV back on.

". . . better than being out on the street," a young man was saying. "If it weren't for her grounding me like that, I'd probably be dead. Now I got my GED, and I'm going to community college to study computers." As the host nodded earnestly, Will's mother withdrew and quietly closed the door behind her.

There was an idea. Maybe if he got his GED, he would never have to go back to school at all.

*   *   *

"Homecoming's over," Coach Laufeld announced. She clapped. "It's time to get to work. We could all use some practice. We were a little sloppy on Saturday. Jessica, I trust you've sufficiently recovered from the homecoming festivities to give us your full concentration?"

Jessica heard Gina and Cherie snicker, and Tia threw her a sympathetic smile. Obviously Laufeld hadn't missed how out of it she was on Saturday. Of course, it would have been hard not to notice. She'd better be a lot sharper today. The wooden floor of the gym was a lot less forgiving.

"We're going to start with a new routine today," Coach Laufeld continued. "I need two rows. You're going to work in pairs. Lila and Jessica, you stand right here, and the rest of you line up behind them."

She's going to be on my case all afternoon, Jessica thought. She glanced out of the corner of her eye at Lila, who ignored her, stone-faced. Lila had been acting semihuman to her lately, but she sure wasn't showing it now.

"Okay. Everybody face your partners. You'll be working in unison, so timing is important. First the footwork. Watch closely." She executed a complicated series of steps. Jessica did her best to concentrate, silently following her coach's movements. *I can do this,* she thought. As long as she didn't think of Jeremy. Or Jade. Or Jeremy and Jade. *Uh-oh,* she thought, realizing she'd missed the last steps of the routine.

"Jessica and Lila will now demonstrate it for the rest of you. Lila, you repeat it as I did it. Jessica, you'll do the mirror image. Let's go."

Jessica turned to face Lila, filled with dread. It was bad enough to screw up on Saturday and get on the coach's bad list. And spacing out on the end had definitely not helped. But to do it in reverse? She might as well just head for the showers now.

"Focus! Okay, let's go."

Jessica managed to keep up with Lila for a half-dozen steps and then got hopelessly lost. *All you have to do is follow Lila,* she thought, trying to calm herself. But she always seemed to be moving in one direction just as Lila took a step in the other, and her lurching efforts to change direction in midstep drew louder and louder laughter from the group.

"Nice work, Lila," Laufeld said when the ordeal was finally over. "Back of the line, you two. Annie and Melissa, you're next." Everyone watched the next group in silence, realizing they would all have to take a turn in front. By the time most of the other pairs had taken a turn, Jessica was confident she'd memorized the routine.

Finally she and Lila were in front again, but this time at least she could handle it.

"Okay, now switch places," Coach Laufeld ordered.

Jessica stifled a groan as she rapidly tried to calculate the opposite of everything she'd just learned.

Lila took her place calmly, and Jessica scrambled to join her.

"One, two, three, four," Laufeld called, clapping out the rhythm. Her head spinning, Jessica managed about three steps correctly before she stepped forward with her left foot just as Lila stepped forward with her right. She landed on Lila's foot.

"Jessica!" snapped Laufeld. "Please try not to step on your partner. Now, one more time, and get it right."

You can do this, Jessica thought. *You've done much harder things a million times. You weren't captain for nothing. Just don't think about—*

"One, two, three, four!" Laufeld chanted. Summoning all her concentration, Jessica launched into her routine. This time it was going perfectly. *I nailed it,* she thought as they neared the end. *And I didn't think of Jeremy once—*

The next thing she knew, she and Lila had collided, and Lila was on the floor, clutching her knee. Coach Laufeld was instantly by her side. "Are you all right?" she asked. "Where does it hurt?"

Lila prodded her knee, wincing, then climbed slowly to her feet. She tested her leg gingerly, then put her weight on it. Jessica could hear angry muttering behind her, and her face was burning. It had been her fault. She had let her mind wander. Laufeld was really going to let her have it. She was a demon about safety.

"Are you all right?" the coach repeated.

Lila nodded.

"What happened?"

Everyone watched Lila, waiting to hear what she would say. She glanced at Jessica, then kicked at the floor.

"Someone should really talk to the custodian about this floor," she muttered. "It's too slippery. I could have hurt myself."

Coach Laufeld raised her eyebrows. "Well, I'll pass that piece of advice right along," she said sarcastically. "If you're okay, then, let's see who's next."

Jessica gaped at Lila as she strolled casually to the back of the line. It had clearly been Jessica's fault. She'd kicked Lila in the knee, hard. And Lila had covered for her. In front of Melissa and her whole crew, who were always waiting for a chance to see Jessica mortified and whose opinions mattered a lot to Lila.

What was going on? First Jade, now Lila. People weren't acting the way she expected. Of course, helping Jade be with Jeremy wasn't exactly typical behavior from *her*. So maybe there was some kind of karmic thing happening.

Or maybe it was time to step back and think about who her friends really were.

Lila Fowler

Maybe I was wrong about Melissa. I thought she always had all the angles covered. But showing up with Ken at the dance on Friday didn't win her any friends. I mean, when your boyfriend is barely out of the hospital and you're already flirting with his main rival, well, people talk.

It really looked like Jessica was no match for Melissa this fall. But I'm not so sure anymore.

And if everyone does run back to Jessica—let's just say I have no intention of getting stuck at the back of the line.

CHAPTER

Ancient History

8

Jessica stretched her arms over her head as she walked out into the parking lot, trying to relax her sore muscles. The cool evening breeze felt good on her face, which was still damp from the locker-room shower. Laufeld had been an absolute demon today. If it weren't for Lila, she would still be in Laufeld's doghouse, but Jessica had pulled it together after her shaky start.

As she approached the corner of the lot where the Jeep was parked, she realized that someone was leaning up against it. She squinted and was pretty sure she could make out Evan's long, grungy hair.

As she got closer, she could tell it was definitely him. When he saw her coming, he stuffed the book he was reading into the pocket of his baggy shorts and waved.

"Evan?" she said, puzzled. Elizabeth had caught a ride with Tia earlier, and since Evan had been monitoring her sister's every move lately, he had to know that. But why would he be waiting for *her?* Unless

Elizabeth had already succeeded in breaking his heart.

"I finished practice early, and I saw your car was here," he explained. "Got a minute?"

"Sure," she said, swinging her backpack and cheerleading bag off her shoulder to rest on the pavement. He smelled like chlorine, as he always did after swimming practice. "So, what's up?" she asked, flashing him her trademark smile.

"I wanted to talk to you about Elizabeth," Evan said bluntly.

"Right," Jessica said, the smile fading. "Elizabeth."

"She's been avoiding me since Friday night. And I think I know why," Evan said.

"Oh?" she said. This was news to her. Of course, she'd hardly spoken to Elizabeth since the dance. They'd managed to get through the entire weekend only exchanging a few words after their fight Saturday morning.

"I know you two haven't been getting along that well lately," Evan said. "And I thought it might be because of me."

Jessica kicked at the ground, not saying anything.

"Well, I was hoping it wouldn't be a big deal," he continued. "Since we've been friends for a while. But I could still see how it might be a little weird for you if Elizabeth and I kind of started hooking up, you know, considering our history."

"Not at all," Jessica said. "It's fine with me." Okay,

she'd given Elizabeth some major heat on this topic. But now that Evan was standing here talking about it, she realized that it really *didn't* bother her if he went out with her sister. The whole thing was kind of annoying, but with so much bigger stuff going on, it barely seemed relevant. Suddenly the way she'd been acting seemed sort of petty.

"I'm not sure Elizabeth knows you feel that way," he said carefully. He leaned back against the door to the Jeep. "She freaks out whenever I'm around," he admitted.

"Ouch," Jessica said. She felt her mouth twitch. "Um, it's maybe *possible* that she did think I had a problem with you guys going out," she said, avoiding his gaze.

"Really?" He paused, flicking fuzz off his shorts. "So, then, do you think you could clear things up with her? Let her know you're okay with it? I mean, as long as you *are* okay with it."

"Of course I am," Jessica almost snapped. "Yeah, I'll talk to her," she said with a sigh.

Why not? I'm getting good at stepping out of the way, she thought. Self-sacrifice seemed to be the theme of the week.

"Thanks, Jessica. You know how Elizabeth is. She worries so much about other people, she forgets to think about herself sometimes."

"Uh-huh. That's Liz, all right," Jessica said, feeling a lump in her throat.

117

"Cool. And thanks, Jessica. See you later." He pushed himself off the car and headed out across the parking lot.

She got in the Jeep and shut the door, sitting there for a moment without turning on the engine. If Evan was right and she was the one standing in the way of Elizabeth and Evan being happy together, then she didn't mind clearing the way. But hearing how self-sacrificing *Elizabeth* was didn't help.

Jeremy glanced at the clock again. Jessica would be arriving in ten minutes. *You're not even going out with the girl,* he thought. He had no right to be this anxious about seeing her.

HOJ was quiet tonight except for some awful CD his coworker Corey had put on. He was itching to put on one of his own instead, but he'd tried that last week and the disc had mysteriously disappeared. When Corey got in one of her moods, there was nothing you could do but ride it out.

About ten people or so were scattered around the café in little knots, and it was so quiet that some of them were actually studying. He found himself wishing for a crowd to come in just so he'd have something to do.

You're not supposed to be bored or lonely. You have a girlfriend, he reminded himself. But it was pointless. He and Jade didn't have that connection, that feeling like there was always a million things you wanted to say.

Like he felt with Jessica.

The whole place always felt different when she was working. Time never seemed to drag when she was around.

But he had to stop thinking like this. Jade needed him now, and for better or worse, he was her boyfriend. Instead of whining about ancient history he should be thinking about how to help Jade. Like, for instance, who did he know who could help find her a job? Maybe over at—

"Hi, Jeremy."

His head jerked up, like he'd been caught doing something wrong—even though he was just organizing the coffee filters. He'd been so absorbed, he hadn't even seen Jessica come in.

"Hey," he said as calmly as he could. She was wearing a cropped black T-shirt that left an inch or two of skin exposed above her low-slung jeans. Jeremy realized he was staring and forced himself to look away.

"I'll be right back," Jessica said, then disappeared into the back office. She came out a minute later and joined him behind the counter, wrapping the apron around her waist.

"Can you help out?" she asked. She turned her back to him and held out the apron strings. Jeremy grasped the strings and tied the knot for her, aware of his knuckles grazing the smooth skin above her belt line.

"Thanks," she said when he'd finished.

"No problem," he said, clearing his throat.

Jessica turned and gave him a big smile. "Hey, congratulations, by the way," she said.

He stared at her, baffled.

"I hear you're winning some academic award. That's great."

"Oh. Yeah, well, I'm just nominated so far."

How did she hear about that?

"I'm sure you'll win, though." She tore open a bag of espresso beans and poured them into the grinder. "Jade is really looking forward to it," Jessica added in what was—even for her—an extremely chipper voice. "She's been so stressed out, so it's nice that you'll have that night together."

Jade? Was he supposed to act like they were all buddies now? Just three old friends? Two weeks ago she and Jade were ready to scratch each other's eyes out.

"Did you hear her mom is home?" Jessica asked. "What a relief, huh? Poor Jade." Jessica reached down into the minifridge and came back up with a container of milk. "Running low," she said.

Jeremy watched her refill the metal pitcher for the cappuccino machine. This was just too weird. This was the same girl who'd dragged him all the way to the beach just to catch Jade with another guy.

Now she seemed more into Jeremy being with Jade than he was.

"So, has it been slow today?" Jessica asked, turning her head as if she couldn't remember what she had to do next. He'd never seen her so hyper. She glanced at him and bit her lip. "You know what, I think I'm gonna check if all the syrups for the Italian sodas are full. Last week the hazelnut ran out right in the middle of a big rush." She pushed a chair beneath the shelf of glass bottles.

"Let me do that," Jeremy said.

"No, I'm fine." Jessica climbed up on the chair and reached for the two bottles on the left—almond and apricot. As she stretched her arms above her head, the bottom of her shirt rose several inches above her waist, exposing an expanse of smooth, tan skin. Jeremy couldn't tear his eyes away. She put them back and reached for another. "This one's almost empty," she said, holding out a bottle of bright yellow liquid. "Banana. Yuck. It must be two years old. Nobody ever drinks it. We should just throw it away."

She held the bottle out toward him, but before he could take it, the bottle slipped from her fingers and shattered on the floor. A strong artificial banana odor immediately filled the room, even overpowering the smell of coffee. Jessica leaned over to see and started to falter on the shaky stool.

"Hold on!" Jeremy said. "Don't jump down. You'll

cut your feet." She was wearing flimsy sandals, and broken glass was everywhere. "Let me get you down. I'm wearing hiking boots."

He stepped over the worst of the mess and took her by the waist. Sparks of electricity flew through him as his fingers touched her skin, but he pushed the sensation away. She put her hands on his shoulders for balance as he lifted her into the air. He carried her a few feet and then set her down on a clean part of the floor.

His hands were still around her waist, and they were only inches apart.

"I'm sorry," she murmured. There was a slight tremble in her voice. "That was so stupid."

"It's okay," he said. "We were going to throw it away anyway, remember?"

She nodded. Her gaze traveled down to her hands on his shoulders, and her cheeks started to flush. His own heart was beating so hard, he could feel it.

He licked his lips, unable to break contact. But she slowly lowered her hands from him, staring up at him with an almost frightened look in her eyes.

"I'd better go get a broom for that," she said, then ran off to the back, leaving Jeremy standing in the hall by himself, his arms still tingling from her touch.

Was he crazy, or was he not the only one who

was having second thoughts about the two of them?

This is so amazing, Jade thought as she burst through the door to House of Java. She ran straight to the counter, dying to share her news with Jeremy. But no one was in sight. She leaned over the counter and saw Jessica wiping something off the floor with a dirty rag.

"Guess what!" she said, feeling like she needed to tell *someone.*

Jessica jumped up. "Jade!" she said. "What are you doing here?" Her face was strangely flushed.

"I got a job!" Jade exclaimed. "Is Jeremy here?"

Jessica wiped her hands on her apron. "Um, I think he's in the back."

"Cool, thanks. I'll see you later." Jade turned and hurried back into the employee lounge.

"Jeremy!" she said, surprised to see him standing alone in the room, just staring into space. "What are you doing back here?"

He blinked. "What are *you* doing here?" he asked.

"I came to see you." She stepped closer and put her arms around his neck, pulling his body against hers. "Is this a bad time?"

"No. You just caught me by surprise, that's all." After hesitating a moment he put his arms loosely around her waist. "What's up?" he asked.

"I just got a job! I went for an interview at Guido's right after school, and they hired me on the spot!"

"That's great," he said, smiling for the first time. "When do you start?"

"Tomorrow! Can you believe it? They just lost two people this week. They were so desperate, they didn't even ask for references." She laughed and squeezed him happily. "I can't believe it. I was such a wreck two days ago, and now everything's fine. My mom's healthy, I got a new job—and I've got you." She inhaled deeply, breathing in his warm scent, then stepped back. "What's that smell?" she asked.

"Oh. Banana syrup," he said, looking away.

"Gross. Don't tell me you like that stuff," Jade said.

"No. See, we, uh, broke it. I must have gotten some on me."

"Well, personally, I'd burn this," Jade said, plucking at the sleeve of his T-shirt. She ran her hands up and down his muscular arms. "I know what I'm going to do with my first paycheck," she murmured, stroking a lock of hair behind his ear.

"What?" he asked.

"Take you out for a nice, romantic dinner."

His smile seemed halfhearted, distracted. He was probably nervous because he was supposed to be working, she realized. Oh, well—that was what she got for having such a responsible, reliable boyfriend. It was kind of cute, actually. But Jessica could handle things out there a while longer.

"As long as we're back here . . . ," Jade whispered. She stood on her tiptoes and slowly brought her lips to his. He didn't respond at first, so she reached her hands back behind his head and pulled it down closer. She kept kissing him, harder, until she felt the rigid muscles in his neck start to relax. He let out a small sigh as he finally sank into the kiss. She pressed her whole body against him.

Then Jade heard the door to the lounge swing open, and Jeremy jerked back from her. She turned to see Jessica standing in the doorway, her eyes widened in shock and . . . something more. There was no way to avoid it—Jessica was in pain. Seeing Jeremy and Jade together hurt her—which meant that Jade had been right all along. Jessica still wanted him.

Before any of them said a word, Jessica spun around and ran back out into the coffeehouse.

Jade turned her attention back to Jeremy, a sinking feeling in her stomach. *Please don't let me see what I think I'm going to see.*

But the look on Jeremy's face was nearly identical to the one she'd just seen on Jessica's. It was like seeing Jessica upset was hurting him worse than being hurt himself. She flashed back in her mind to the moment on the beach when Jeremy had caught her kissing Josh Radinsky. He'd been shocked, yeah. But he hadn't seemed destroyed, the way he did now.

Feeling tears sting the backs of her eyelids, she blinked rapidly. "Looks like you're wanted out front," she said as casually as she could. "I'd better let you go before I get you in trouble. So I'll see you tomorrow night, okay?" She gave him a quick kiss on the cheek, then turned and rushed out. She walked quickly through the main room, carefully avoiding glancing in Jessica's direction.

As soon as she was outside, she let herself break into a run to get to her car. Her feet pounded on the pavement. What was she thinking? How had she convinced herself that Jeremy could care about her? He was as hung up on Jessica as she was on him. The two of them just couldn't admit it.

She slowed as she reached her car, panting. Okay, maybe Jeremy had feelings for Jessica. But what was she supposed to do? Give up and slink away in humiliation? That wasn't exactly her style. Even if there was still something between them, she had nothing to lose by fighting it out.

So what if Jeremy wasn't all the way over Jessica yet—that didn't necessarily mean she was any more right for him than Jade was. If he'd met Jade first, it could have been the other way around.

All she had to do was give Jeremy more time to get over Jessica. Then she'd *make* him fall for her.

Jade deserved a good guy like Jeremy. And now that she was this close to having him, she wasn't going to let him go.

Jessica Wakefield

Okay, okay. Calm down.

What did Evan say? Empty your mind. Find your center.

Ommm.

Ommm.

Ommm.

Oh my God.

I can't believe I'm sitting here in the bathroom at HOJ, reciting a nonsense syllable.

So much for meditation.

Evan doesn't know what he's talking about.

CHAPTER

Rotten Bananas

9

Elizabeth hadn't even realized she had zoned out until the sound of the front door slamming downstairs jolted her out of her trance.

She focused in on the phone lying on her desk in front of her. She'd been spending the whole afternoon trying to figure out if she wanted it to ring or *didn't* want it to ring. She'd never really made up her mind, but it wasn't like it mattered anyway. It hadn't rung.

"Jessica?" Elizabeth called out as she heard footsteps coming up the stairs. She wished they could end this stupid fight already. She was tired of missing everyone. She got up and walked to her doorway. Jessica stood at the top of the stairs, her entire face seeming to *droop*.

"Hey," Elizabeth said, walking toward her. "What's wrong?"

Jessica glanced up at her and sighed. She sank down onto the floor of the hallway, slipping off her sandals and rubbing her feet. "Just tired," she muttered.

But Elizabeth knew her sister better than that. "Did something happen?" she pressed.

Jessica didn't answer.

Elizabeth bit her lip. "I'm sorry. Do you want to be alone?"

"I'm fine, really," Jessica said. "Actually, I do need to talk to you." She gestured at the floor, and Elizabeth sat down next to her. "It's about Evan."

Elizabeth stiffened. *Not again. I don't know how much more of this I can take.*

"I wanted to apologize," Jessica continued.

"What?" Elizabeth sat up, startled. "Why?"

"Well, I haven't exactly been *mature* about the whole thing," Jessica said, picking at the hem of her T-shirt.

Elizabeth paused. "You were upset," she said. "It's okay."

"No, really. I was just being selfish. If you and Evan are good together, that's great. I shouldn't feel so possessive about someone I'm not even going out with." She slumped lower and rested her chin in her hand, staring at the wall.

"You weren't being selfish," Elizabeth argued. "You were just telling me what I told you before. And the more I've thought about it, the more I realized you had a point." She hadn't even known it was true until she said it, but it was.

"What do you mean?" Jessica asked, frowning.

"It was crazy of me to rush into something so

fast. I was just going to get all of us hurt—me, Evan, maybe even Conner. If he actually cares at all," she couldn't help adding under her breath.

"Are you sure about this?" Jessica asked.

Elizabeth nodded. "Evan's great, but I'm not ready for another relationship. Not like he is. It just isn't fair."

"If that's what you want, okay," Jessica said. "I have to warn you—Evan's already in pretty deep." Elizabeth cringed. "But in case you change your mind, it's totally cool with me if you guys go out."

"Thanks, Jess," Elizabeth said. She leaned forward to give her twin a hug. "I'm so glad you're not mad anymore."

"I've had a lot of practice with this self-sacrificing thing lately," Jessica replied after they pulled back. "I guess I'm getting good at it." She sighed again. "So, what are you going to do?"

"I don't know," Elizabeth said. "But I think I'll be okay. It was ten times worse when I couldn't talk to you about it." She stood up. "Are you sure there's nothing you wanted to talk about? You really don't look too happy."

Jessica shook her head. "Just tired from work."

Elizabeth was pretty sure that was a lie, but she wasn't going to push it. She had her sister back after the first major fight they'd had in a while. That was enough for now.

Jessica Wakefield

No matter how I feel right now, it was probably good for me to see them like that. Sometimes you need to have your face really rubbed in something before you believe it's true. And that was my wake-up call.

I mean, I <u>knew</u> Jeremy and Jade were together, but it was like part of me didn't believe it. Way in the back of my mind I was clinging to this fantasy that he really wanted me, not her.

Well, I'm over that. You don't kiss someone like that unless you really mean it.

But at least I finally got the message. All I have to do is make it official — find one last way to convince that tiny, pathetic part of myself that I'm okay with them being together. People would think I was crazy, but I have to do this. And besides, having Jade as a friend again wouldn't be so bad. So here I go on my absolutely _last_ self-sacrificial quest of the week. I swear.

"Mom!" Jade exclaimed as she walked into the kitchen. "You shouldn't be doing that."

"I'm fine," her mother said. But Jade still rushed over and took the heavy pot of water from her hands, placing it on the stove herself.

Ms. Wu did look a lot better. She had seemed pretty weak when she'd gotten out of the hospital, but now she was moving around like her old self. Still, there was no point in pushing it. "Can I help with something?" Jade asked.

Her mother shook her head firmly and turned on the stove. "How was your day?" she asked.

"Great," Jade lied, picturing the horrified expression on Jeremy's face. "I got a job today!" Jade took the head of lettuce lying on the counter and started washing it over the sink. "I'm going to be a hostess at Guido's. They hired me on the spot."

Her mother's body visibly relaxed, filling Jade with relief. She'd finally done something to help her mom feel better.

"I wasn't worried," Ms. Wu said. She turned to give her daughter a smile. "You've always succeeded when you really wanted something."

Did that apply to Jeremy too? If she was determined enough to really fight for him, would she win? Normally Jade talked about this stuff with her mom, but she didn't want her to have to worry about anything else right now.

The doorbell rang, and Jade quickly dried her

hands on the dish towel. "I'll get it," she said. She hurried over to the front door, telling herself that she wasn't hoping it was Jeremy.

"Who is it?" she called through the door.

"Um, it's Jessica Wakefield."

Not Jeremy.

"Jessica?" She frowned. Did this mean she was going to have to start fighting for Jeremy sooner than she'd thought? She pulled open the door, giving Jessica a weak smile. "Hey, come on in," she said.

Jessica followed her into the living room, and they sat down on the couch. Jade crossed and then uncrossed her legs. Beads of sweat formed on her palms.

"Something smells great," Jessica said.

"Yeah. My mom's cooking," Jade said. Actually, what she smelled right now was more like . . . rotten bananas. The way Jeremy had smelled earlier.

"I'm so glad she's doing better," Jessica said.

"What? Oh, yeah, me too," Jade said.

Get to the point! The longer it took for Jessica to just say why she was here, the faster Jade's heart raced.

Jessica cleared her throat. "I was cleaning up my dresser tonight," she said. "And I saw this." She reached into her purse and pulled out a silver necklace. "It's just like the one you used to have, the one you wanted to wear to the banquet." She handed it to Jade. "I thought maybe you'd want to borrow it."

Jade slowly reached out and took the necklace. That was it? That's what she'd come here for? She twisted the necklace in her hands, watching the narrow strands shimmer. Jade stared into Jessica's eyes, searching for an explanation. "Why are you doing this?" she blurted out.

Jessica glanced away. "I can tell that you and Jeremy are really happy," she said. Jade noticed that she was twisting her hands together in her lap. Her knuckles were almost white. "I want to make it clear that I'm okay with that," she continued. "From now on, I promise to stay out of it."

"Oh," Jade said, her mind whirling. Why was Jessica being so nice? Didn't she know they were supposed to be rivals?

Jessica stood up. "I should get home," she said. "I'm exhausted."

"So you came all the way over here just to give me this?" Jade asked, holding up the necklace. "And to tell me that, um, that you know Jeremy and I belong together?" Her tongue felt thick as she said the words. They sounded so wrong—especially saying them to Jessica. Jessica nodded, but it was obvious how strained the motion was.

"That's really nice of you," Jade said. "I mean, *really* nice." *Too nice.* Things were much simpler when they had been fighting. How was she supposed to mount an all-out struggle for Jeremy if the girl wasn't fighting back?

"It's no big deal," Jessica said. "But I really should go," she added, glancing toward the front door.

They stood and walked to the door together. Jade felt like there was something else she was supposed to say, but she wasn't sure what. This just wasn't a situation she was used to—a *girl* being a good friend to her.

After she closed the door behind Jessica, she stood there for a minute, twisting the necklace in her hands. Obviously this was because of the incident at HOJ today. The kiss. But why would that make Jessica do this?

Jade tried to put herself in Jessica's place. She'd walked in on the guy she liked making out with someone else. So now she was trying to show she didn't care, the way Jade probably would have done. She didn't want to make a fool of herself because she thought Jeremy was totally over her and into Jade.

Except he wasn't. Jessica hadn't seen his face afterward.

So what now? If Jade was the only one who knew how everyone *really* felt, was it totally evil not to just let them be together?

TIA RAMIREZ

DEAR CONNER:

HOW'S IT GOING?

GOD, IT'S ROUGH NOT HAVING YOU AROUND. AND WHAT MAKES IT TEN TIMES WORSE IS, USUALLY IF SOMETHING'S BUGGING ME, YOU'RE THE ONE I TALK TO ABOUT IT. SO WHEN YOU'RE NOT HERE, I END UP MISSING YOU TWICE.

BUT I KNOW WHAT I'M GOING THROUGH IS NOTHING COMPARED TO WHAT YOU'RE DEALING WITH RIGHT NOW. THE LAST THING YOU PROBABLY NEED IS SOME DEPRESSING LETTER ABOUT HOW LONELY AND UNHAPPY I AM.

WELL, YOU DON'T HAVE TO WORRY. THIS ONE IS GOING IN THE TRASH CAN WITH ALL THE OTHERS.

I MISS YOU, CONNER.

OH, WELL. SEE YOU LATER.

LOVE, TEE

"Are you sick, sweetie?"

Jade glanced up at her mother, who was watching Jade's plate with a frown. Most of her food was still uneaten, and she'd just been moving it around with her fork.

"No, I'm just not that hungry," Jade replied.

"Now that I'm working fewer hours, I'll be able to cook dinner more," Ms. Wu said. "I'm sorry I haven't always been able to do that."

"You were working fifteen-hour days, Mom!" Jade objected. "I don't see how you got done everything you did. I can cook my own dinner."

Jade shook her head as she imagined her mother getting home from her second job late at night and instead of going to sleep, cooking a meal for Jade to eat the next day. It was unbelievable. And she'd just taken it all for granted.

Her mother smiled at her. "You don't understand. I love you, Jade. It makes me happy to do things for you."

Jade pursed her lips. Her mother was just so *good* to her. First Jessica and now her mom. It was like the world was trying to let her know what a terrible person she was.

"Listen to me, Jade. When you love somebody, what makes you happy is what makes that person happy. I know I've been pushing myself too hard, and I'm going to cut down—for both of our sakes. But you have to understand that I'm not doing anything I don't want to do. Raising you has been the most fulfilling part of my life."

Jade squirmed on the hard wooden chair. "But what about you, Mom? What about you being happy?"

Ms. Wu smiled and reached across the table to cover Jade's hand with her own. "I am happy," she insisted. "There's nothing more satisfying than being able to do things for the people you love. You'll see."

Jade stared at her mother. Wasn't love supposed to make you both feel happy just from being together? Wasn't it about needing the other person?

But it wasn't like she was any expert on love. She'd never kidded herself she was in love with any of the guys she dated. It was always about having a good time.

At least—until she met Jeremy. It was different with Jeremy. This time she wanted a real relationship.

But if she cared about him that much, shouldn't she want what was best for him, like her mom was saying? That's what Jessica was doing—stepping aside to let Jeremy be with Jade since that's what she thought he wanted.

"Jade?" her mother said, interrupting her thoughts. "Are you sure you don't want anything else before I clean up?"

"No, thanks. I'm full. It was really good," she added. She stood up and started to clear the table. She wasn't happy about it—but she knew what she had to do next.

To: marsden1@swiftnet.com
From: mslater@swiftnet.com
Subject: re: *Oracle* article

Andy,
   Great job! I can't wait to show the school there are so many more important things going on here than just football. Isn't it ridiculous how hyped everyone got over the stupid homecoming game? Please. So Ken got five touchdown passes. Whatever. But I love your article—it rocks!

CHAPTER
making Progress
10

Ken strode confidently into Mr. Nelson's office, smiling as he remembered how nervous he'd been during his first appointment earlier in the fall. Back then he'd just quit the team, and he'd plunged from certain NCAA-division-I scholarship material to the bottom of the academic food chain. They'd gone over his grades together, and when he realized that a string of highly unimpressive letters would be the only summary of all his accomplishments in the last four years, he'd broken out into a cold sweat.

He had left the room that day envisioning a future of pumping gas or dunking baskets of fries into a bubbling vat of hot oil. This time, though, things were different.

"Nice to see you, Ken," Mr. Nelson greeted him as he walked in. "Have a seat."

Ken sat down across from Mr. Nelson, who was thumbing through a manila folder. He casually crossed his legs and threw his arm over the back of his chair. Last time Ken had felt like he was sitting down for a job interview where he was completely unqualified. This time he felt more like a celebrity guest on *David Letterman*.

Mr. Nelson nodded repeatedly as he flipped through the papers. "You've made real progress as far as your grades are concerned. That's very good. As I said last time, when there are questions about the overall record, sometimes an upward trend in the last year will make an admissions officer give you the benefit of the doubt." He looked up at Ken and smiled. "Your hard work has been paying off."

"Thanks," Ken said. Maybe this wouldn't take too long, and he could duck outside for a doughnut before going back to class.

"I do want to remind you, however, that it's important to maintain your grades at this level over the entire year. Often after I meet with someone, there is a burst of action, then after a month or so they backslide. The key is good study habits, to set up a schedule." He stared at Ken expectantly over the glasses perched on his nose.

"Yeah, I was doing that for a while," he said.

"And then?"

And then I broke up with Maria, Ken thought. "I haven't had as much time to study since I started playing football again." He shrugged. What difference did it make? He wouldn't have to worry about his grades anymore.

"Hmmm. I hope you don't feel like it's a choice between one or the other, Ken. Colleges like to see a healthy balance between academics and extracurricular activities."

Oh, right, like Krubowski is really concerned about my history quiz tomorrow, Ken thought, trying not to smile. "To be honest," he said, "I'm not too concerned about getting into college anymore."

"Oh? Why is that?"

"'Cause they're all recruiting me now," he said. What was with this guy? Hadn't he heard about the game Saturday? It had been in all the papers.

Mr. Nelson's brow furrowed. "I'm sure I don't have to tell you that football will take you only so far in life," he said. "It's a whole different world once you enter the workplace. It's never too early to start thinking about a career, Ken."

A career? Ken thought. It would be more than four years before he had to worry about getting a job. Four years of being cheered by crowds of seventy thousand . . .

"All right, Ken?"

Apparently he had missed something Mr. Nelson had said while he was daydreaming. Oh, well. It couldn't have been that important.

"Uh-huh. Can I go now?" Ken asked, starting to rise from his seat. He really wasn't in the mood to deal with a lecture from this guy who obviously had no clue what the sports world was about. Mr. Nelson was probably just jealous. It must be depressing, spending his whole life working at this little job just to see kids like Ken pass him by.

Mr. Nelson tapped his fingertips together and looked down at the folder, frowning. "Ken, you realize that even athletes are required to maintain passing grades in college. I just want to make sure you're not being . . . overconfident."

Ken shook his head. "Definitely not," he said. "In fact, I'm ready right now. I can't wait for college."

"Let's just get you graduated from high school first, okay?" Mr. Nelson said, shutting his folder with a sigh.

"Yeah, okay," Ken said. "See you later," he said as he walked out the door. He really *couldn't* wait for college. People took their football seriously at Michigan. He wouldn't have to waste so much time with stuff like this.

Ken glanced at his watch. A few more hours and he'd be back on the practice field.

Elizabeth stumbled out of her history class, feeling like she hadn't even been there. The whole lecture had just been a blur. If she couldn't borrow somebody's notes, she was in trouble.

She made her way to her locker and unlocked it on the third try, only to find she'd left her math book at home. She shut her eyes and leaned against her locker door. This was going to be a long day.

"Elizabeth?"

Despite all of her determination to be strong, she felt her heart squeeze at the sound of his voice. She opened her eyes and saw him standing there, holding out a cup of coffee.

"I thought you could use this," he said, handing it to her.

"Thanks," she said. How did he *always* know exactly what she needed? It made everything so much harder.

Evan stepped forward, his eyes questioning. She held her breath as he came closer and reached out to put his hands on her shoulders. It was so *easy* letting him hold her.

Evan's face was just inches away. Suddenly her mind cleared, and she remembered what she had to say. If she kept jerking him around, she'd only make things worse for both of them.

"I'm sorry," she said, meeting his gaze directly for what felt like the first time in a while. "But I can't be with you. Not the way you want. I'm just going through too much right now."

"I *know* what you're going through," he said. "And I don't mind. I want to be with you, to help you through it. That's all I want."

"I know. But I can't be there for *you*," she argued.

"I can wait," he said. "I'm not in a hurry." He moved his hand to her chin, tilting it upward.

He knew she was still a mess about Conner. And he didn't mind. He really cared about her. So who was she doing a favor by pushing him away? Him? Her?

She backed away, letting his hands fall away from

her. "Evan—no," she said firmly. "It's just not right. I'm really sorry. I do care about you, but the timing . . ."

He nodded, then wiped a hand over his mouth. "No, I get it," he said. He forced a small smile. "I guess I'm just destined to be the Wakefield sisters' rebound guy."

Elizabeth winced.

"Sorry," Evan said immediately. "I didn't mean that to sound so obnoxious." He paused. "Listen, I'm not going to lie here. I wanted things to be more with us. A lot. And I think it could have been something. But if it's not what you want, I'm not going to push. And I hope we can still be friends."

She nodded.

"Good. So, enjoy the coffee," he said, pointing at the cup she held in her hands. "And I'll see you around." He kissed her lightly on the cheek, then walked away.

Elizabeth felt all the air go out of her, and she slumped against her locker.

Well, you did it, she thought. So shouldn't she feel proud or relieved? Instead all she felt was exhausted . . . and alone.

"So," Mr. Nelson began as soon as Melissa had settled into her chair. "Last time you were here, you were talking about applying to USC, I believe?"

Melissa nodded. That felt like forever ago. A separate senior year from the one she was living now.

"I think that sounds like a good fit for you. They have an excellent communications program. Where else have you been considering?"

Melissa squirmed. Once Will had gotten his heart set on Michigan, she'd thrown out all her other applications. Now she was back at square one. But Mr. Nelson was waiting.

"Um, I was thinking of Michigan," she said.

"The University of Michigan?" Mr. Nelson's eyebrows jumped up. "Any particular reason?"

She bit her lip.

"Don't get me wrong—it's a fine school," he added. "It has several excellent departments. I was just under the impression you wanted to stay closer to home. Was there something specific that attracted you there?"

"Not really," Melissa said. "Just that my—some friends were thinking of going there, and it sounded like a good place."

"Okay. Fine." He clasped his hands and set them on his mahogany desk. "I think what you need to do now is make a list of five or six possibilities and then do a little research. We've got a big collection of catalogs here in the career-resource center, and you can write away for more information from any that interest you. And of course with schools like UCLA and USC, you can arrange a personal tour with one of their guides."

"Arrange one?" Melissa asked. "You mean, all by myself?"

"As long as you call ahead, you shouldn't have any problem making an appointment," said Mr. Nelson. "You can get the phone numbers in their catalogs."

"Isn't there a group that goes together from SVH or something?" she asked.

"No," he replied. He cocked his head at her. "But remember, we won't be there to help you next year, so it's good preparation for doing things on your own."

She felt her cheeks get hot. Was he calling her a baby? Who wouldn't be a little freaked out at the idea of going off alone to walk through a campus filled with thousands of strangers? Especially after thinking that she'd be starting college with Will at her side . . .

Melissa wrapped her arms around herself. *I don't know if I can do this. How am I supposed to choose some random school by myself?*

"I think now would be a good time to look through some catalogs," Mr. Nelson said, rising from his chair. "I'll show you where we keep everything."

Melissa followed him into an adjoining room, where boxes of college catalogs were arranged in a row on a table. He pulled out a chair for her. "I'll leave you in here," he said. "Let me know if you need anything." He went back into his office, leaving Melissa alone.

She looked at the boxes filled with colorful booklets, each one representing an entirely different future. There were hundreds of them. Where was she supposed to begin? She looked through the box marked *M–P* until she found the familiar blue Michigan seal. At least this one she had seen before—it wasn't like looking at a foreign country. She flipped through the pages. The campus looked pretty. And everyone looked happy.

In the middle was a huge, full-page picture of Michigan at the Rose Bowl. A sea of fans dressed in blue were cheering like crazy as the football team ran onto the field. And there were the cheerleaders. The uniforms weren't bad. And they looked nice. She could do that.

Imagine cheering in front of all those people. And on national TV. They always liked to cut to the cheerleaders before going to a commercial. She could watch some games this year and see what they looked for, the best places to stand and stuff like that. It was usually pretty easy to figure out how to get picked for things because no one else paid as close attention to the important details as she did. She smiled. Maybe it was just because she was used to the idea already, but Michigan didn't seem as scary as just picking some random place out of a box.

She closed the pamphlet and set it on the table. Going there with Will would have been so perfect. But with his injury he didn't have a chance at being recruited by Michigan. Krubowski had already forgotten all about him. He was completely focused on Ken now.

Suddenly she sat up straight. Maybe her Michigan fantasy could still come true after all. If Ken ended up going to Michigan—and she was going out with Ken—then everything could still work. She would still be the cheerleading girlfriend of the star quarterback. It would just be a different quarterback.

She breathed a sigh of relief. It was still a long shot, but at least now she had a plan. And it sure beat starting out somewhere as a complete unknown, another face in the crowd. A nobody. She shivered. That would be a nightmare. She definitely couldn't handle that.

Mr. Nelson stuck his head in the door. "Making any progress?" he asked.

"Yes. I think I am," she said, standing up. She slipped the Michigan catalog into her notebook and followed him out of the room.

"One! Two! Three! Four!" As Coach Laufeld clapped out the beat, Jessica went through the steps of the new routine on autopilot. She had it totally down now—her body had taken over. But it was getting harder and harder to remember a time when she had actually thought this was fun.

What made it worse was that every time she looked up, Jade kept smiling at her. As if Jessica needed a reminder that Jade was going to Jeremy's banquet with him tonight and that she'd been the one to make it all happen.

The drill ended, and Jessica stood with her hands on her hips, staring down at the thick painted lines on the floor.

"Nice work, girls," Coach Laufeld said. Jessica

looked up to see her nodding in satisfaction. "See you all tomorrow."

Before Tia or anyone else could come talk to her, Jessica hurried out of the gym and headed for the locker room. If she showered fast enough, she could be out of there without having to deal with Jade's happy expression or Tia's sympathetic one.

"Wait!" Footsteps pounded behind her. Jessica slowed, gritting her teeth. Jade ran up and fell in beside her. "Tough workout, huh?" she said, catching her breath.

"Yeah," Jessica agreed. Why couldn't Jade just let things go?

"Look, Jessica, I wanted to ask you something. You know that banquet I'm going to with Jeremy tonight?"

Jessica tried not to roll her eyes. "Uh-huh," she said patiently. *Like I'm really going to forget when you've thanked me for the necklace three times today,* she thought.

"Well, are you free tonight?" Jade asked.

Jessica stopped walking and glanced at Jade in confusion. "Why?" she asked.

"I have a favor to ask. It's for Jeremy, actually. He has a friend who needed a date, last minute. I told him I'd bring someone."

Jessica started walking again, trying to stifle her anger. Like it wasn't bad enough just knowing they were out together—now Jade expected her to sit there and watch? "I don't think so," she said.

"But I promised him," Jade said, biting her lip. "I think it's really important to him."

"Why don't you ask someone else, then?" Jessica asked. She'd been finally starting to think Jade wasn't so evil after all. But asking her to do this was pretty low.

"I did," Jade said. They walked into the locker room, and Jade followed Jessica over to her locker. "But no one wanted to go out to Big Mesa to some dinner where they wouldn't know anyone. I figured since you've been there before and you and Jeremy are such good friends . . . he'd be really happy if you came," Jade said. "I'll never ask for anything again, I promise."

This is not happening, Jessica thought. How much more of this martyr stuff was she expected to take? She shook her head. "Sorry," she said.

"Jess, it would mean a *lot* to Jeremy," Jade said. "I know it sounds weird, but can you just trust me on this?"

Jessica narrowed her eyes at Jade, noticing that Jade's expression was way more serious than usual. She didn't know why, but it was obviously really important that she show up at this thing. How could she keep saying no when Jade made it sound like it would destroy Jeremy?

"Okay," she said. "I guess I could make it. What time?"

"Great!" Jade said. "We're all meeting on the front steps of Big Mesa at seven. See you there." She gave Jessica a mysterious smile. "You'll be glad you came, I promise." Before Jessica could ask any more questions, Jade turned and dashed off to her locker.

Maria Slater

<u>Oracle</u> <u>Editorial</u>

In a season already filled with stirring ~~hype~~ victories, this year's homecoming game reached a whole new level of ~~nauseating self-congratulation~~ achievement. With a rousing 48–14 victory, the SVH squad gave the capacity crowd of ~~pathetically~~ sports-crazed alumni something to gloat about ~~in the bars~~ with their families for years to come.

Led by ~~a shallow, fickle, narcissistic quarterback~~ an unstoppable offense that marched up and down the field ~~like tin soldiers~~ virtually at will, the undefeated home team had the crowd cheering ~~like bloodthirsty zombies~~ deliriously from beginning to end, with a homecoming record five touchdown passes by their all-conference quarterback, Ken Matthews.

We at the *Oracle* would like to ~~vomit~~ join all of you in congratulating our team on their ~~utterly groundless hero status,~~

~~especially considering they consist of~~
~~nothing but a bunch of self-~~
~~important, beefed up halfwits with~~
~~swelled heads the size of Mount~~
~~Rushmore, who all seem to believe~~
~~they're entitled to the adoration of~~
~~their smarter, more accomplished~~
~~classmates solely because they have~~
~~perfected the intricate art of~~
~~slamming into each other at full speed~~
success.

CHAPTER
11
Second Chances

Jeremy zipped up his pants, then ran a hand through his wet hair. That shower had felt almost as good as practice had. A hard workout without a girl in sight had been exactly what he needed.

There was nothing like a crossing pattern to focus the mind—running across midfield right through the heart of the defense, knowing he was going to get hit. After four days of thinking about Jade and Jessica nonstop, it was a relief to have all thoughts pounded out of him by the Big Mesa defensive backs. He would gladly trade a few bruises tomorrow for the feeling he had right now—too tired to worry about anything.

"Ready to head out?" Trent asked, walking up to him with his gym bag slung over one shoulder.

Jeremy nodded. "Let's go," he said. He hoisted his own bag over his arm and followed his friend out of the locker room.

They walked out the side door to the parking lot, and Jeremy blinked when he felt the hot air hit him. It was a muggy day, with terrible smog. He'd been sweating nonstop all practice, and although he'd stood under the shower for about fifteen minutes, he was already starting to sweat again. He'd have to put on the air-conditioning in the car, or he'd need another shower before the banquet.

The banquet. Okay—there went not thinking about Jade.

He walked with Trent across the parking lot in silence. That was the good thing about guys. They didn't talk unless they had something to say.

They reached Jeremy's old Mercedes, and he dropped his bag on the asphalt and turned to Trent. "I guess I'll see you later," he said.

"Yeah, okay. Doing anything fun tonight?"

Right. Fun.

"I've got this academic banquet later," Jeremy said, gesturing at the school building. He leaned back against the car door and crossed his arms over his chest.

"Oh, right!" Trent broke into a grin. "I'm glad you're keeping up with the academics because no one's giving you a football scholarship."

Jeremy laughed. "Maybe," he said. "But who wants to hang out with a bunch of dumb jocks anyway, right?"

Trent faked a punch, and Jeremy ducked out of the way.

"So I guess you're not up for a bite or something before you head home?" Trent asked.

"No." Jeremy stuck his hand in his pocket to get his car keys. "I have to get changed for this thing. I'm picking up Jade at . . ." He trailed off as he noticed a familiar figure heading toward them across the parking lot.

What was *she* doing here?

I got here just in time, Jade thought. She could see Jeremy talking to Trent on the other side of the parking lot by Jeremy's car. *Good. Trent's there too,* she thought.

They both looked over at her, and she waved. Trent waved back, but Jeremy just stared at her. She jogged over. She'd have to handle this just right. It was lucky that Trent was there—he gave her the perfect way to accomplish her plan.

"Hi, guys," she said. "How was practice?"

"Hey, Jade," Trent said. He turned to Jeremy. "See you later, Aames."

"What's the rush?" Jade asked, glancing up at him with a big smile. "I just got here."

"Yeah, well, I figured you and Aames would want some quality time," he said, grinning at Jeremy.

"How do you know I'm here to see him?" Jade asked, widening her smile. Trent frowned, then gave Jeremy an uncertain glance. Jade laughed. "Don't get nervous. I'm just kidding." She stood on tiptoe and kissed Jeremy on the cheek. He did not look happy.

"So, Trent," she said, clutching Jeremy's arm. "How did our boy do in practice today?"

"Not too bad," he said. "He took a beating out there, though. I'm sure he'll offer to show you his bruises later."

"What about you? Are you going to show me yours?"

she asked, her voice low and purposely flirtatious.

"Jade . . . ," Jeremy started.

"Is that what you guys do in the locker room?" she asked Trent, ignoring Jeremy. "Compare bruises to see whose is bigger?"

Trent snorted. "I'm not touching that one. You're on your own, Aames. See ya, Jade."

She waved and smiled coyly as he strode off.

"Are you finished?" Jeremy asked once they were alone.

"What?" Jade asked innocently.

"Don't you ever stop?" he asked. "Do you flirt with every guy you see?"

"What are you talking about?" She flipped her hair back over her shoulder, avoiding his gaze.

"Well, if that's how you act in front of me to my friend, I'd hate to see what happens when I'm not there."

"What are you saying?" Jade asked. "You don't trust me?"

His eyes narrowed. "Should I?"

She gazed up at him, wishing somehow that she could stop all of this. She'd thought it would make it easier if she gave him a reason—an excuse—to let go of her. But she couldn't handle him thinking she was really so awful.

She looked down at the ground, focusing on smoothing out every wrinkle in her linen skirt.

"Look, what are you doing here anyway?" Jeremy asked. She flinched at the angry tone in his voice.

"Why are you with me?" she asked softly. She raised

her eyes back up to meet his. She'd come here determined to break up, to send him on his way to Jessica. But suddenly she was dying to hear him fight for her, to hear him tell her that she was the one he wanted, not Jessica. "Jeremy, do you really want to be with me?"

He looked away. That was all the information she needed.

"Then what are we doing?" she demanded. "I mean, yeah, it was nice of you to come over when my mom was in the hospital . . . but why are you acting like we're a couple when that's not what you want?"

He shuffled his feet, then moved his gaze back to her. His eyes were full of guilt, but nothing more. He didn't care about her, not like she cared about him. She squeezed her car keys in her hand until her palm started to burn.

"Maybe you're right," he said. "Maybe this isn't working. I just—I do like you a lot, Jade. And I know how rough things are for you right—" He must have seen her wince because he stopped.

"I'm not looking for pity," she said coldly.

"Yeah, I know. Jade, I'm sorry. Really."

"There's nothing to be sorry about," she said with a forced smile. She took a deep breath, trying not to focus on his sweet, warm eyes or the lips she knew felt impossibly soft on her skin. . . .

"Good-bye, Jeremy," she said. She turned just in time to keep him from seeing her face crack into tears and walked away.

*   *   *

Not bad, Ken thought as he checked out his reflection in the locker-room mirror. He ran the comb through his hair one more time. Those Michigan girls would be flocking around him like bees to honey. And he'd have four long years to enjoy them. Five if they redshirted him.

Coach Riley stuck his head in the locker-room door. "Matthews," he called out. "Don't forget to come by my office. Krubowski's waiting."

Yes. As if he could have forgotten. He'd sailed through this entire day, waiting for the moment when Hank Krubowski offered him a full ride to Michigan.

Ken threw his comb in the bag with his clothes and followed Coach Riley out, then down the hall into his office.

"Hello, Ken."

Ken recognized the deep, gravelly voice instantly. He glanced over and saw Hank Krubowski standing next to Coach Riley's desk with his arms crossed. Even slouching, he towered over both Ken and his coach.

"Mr. Krubowski. Nice to see you." Ken glanced from his coach back to the Michigan scout, trying to read their stone faces. Was this it? Was he going to get the offer now? It was still a little early in the year to ask him to sign a letter of intent—they must really be afraid of losing him.

"I was just talking to your coach, Ken," Mr. Krubowski said. He motioned toward one of the plush chairs in front of the desk, and Ken sat down.

Coach Riley walked around them and sank into his chair, but Mr. Krubowski remained standing.

"I'm going to be blunt, Ken," Mr. Krubowski began. "I've been watching you for a couple of weeks now. There's no question in my mind that you've got a division-I arm. Michigan's been scouting you since your junior year, and everyone who's seen you agrees you've got real talent." Ken held back a grin. This was it—this was really it.

"But I'm concerned about your absence from the team this fall," Mr. Krubowski continued.

Ken shifted in his seat. What did that have to do with anything? He was back now and playing great.

"Your coach explained that you were going through some tough times." Mr. Krubowski peered down at him as if considering whether he would make a good chew toy for his dog. "But anytime a player quits during the season, that's a major, major point of concern."

Ken shot an anxious glance at his coach. What exactly had he told him? The windowless basement office suddenly seemed more dungeonlike than ever.

"I just don't know, Ken. You have obvious potential—physically. But the game of football is fifty percent mental. It takes guts. You've got to be willing to stick it out, no matter how tough it gets."

"I am," Ken blurted out. "That was a onetime thing. I swear, it will never happen again. It was just that with the earthquake—"

Mr. Krubowski leaned back against Coach Riley's

metal desk. "Everybody else on the team went through the same earthquake, didn't they?" Ken stared at him, amazed. How could he even say that? His girlfriend had *died* in that quake. His coach must have told him what happened.

"I know it's easy to get swept away by your emotions, Ken." There was a hint of disgust in his voice. "But quarterback is a leadership position. The whole team looks to you to rally them when the going gets tough." He leaned toward Ken. "Our goal at Michigan every year is to win the championship. We're looking for a leader who will hang in there no matter what happens. It's not a position for quitters, Ken."

"I'm not a quitter," Ken said, balling his hands into fists.

"Do you think you've got problems, Ken? You should see some of the neighborhoods I recruit in. I've got kids on my team with no parents, brothers in jail. Guys who've seen their best friends get shot right in front of them. Guys with *real* problems. And you know what? Not one of those guys has yet to miss a single day of practice." He straightened. "If every player who was having problems with his girlfriend decided to stay home on Saturday, we wouldn't be able to field a team."

Ken felt his skin burn. Problems with his girlfriend? A person had died. Didn't that mean anything to him?

"I said I'd be honest with you. The jury's still out on you, Ken. We'll be watching you closely the rest of the season. But we want only winners on our team. If you want to play for Michigan, you're going to have to show you're a little more serious about the game of football. I'd like to offer you a scholarship, but the next month will really be your chance to prove you can handle it."

He shook hands with Coach Riley and Ken, then left the room.

Ken glanced at his coach, dazed. What had just happened here? Was he on some kind of *probation* or something?

Coach Riley pursed his lips. "I told you, you still have a lot to prove, Ken. You're lucky to be considered by Michigan at all."

Ken felt too numb to answer. A few minutes ago it had seemed like such a sure thing. His scholarship had been in the bag.

"I'm sorry," his coach said. "But I had to be honest with him. If you quit on your teammates, no matter how talented you are, it's a black mark you'll carry with you forever."

What *had* his coach told Krubowski? It didn't sound like he'd exactly given him a glowing character reference.

"You've still got a chance, Ken. They wouldn't keep watching you if you weren't in the running. But there's a lot of talent out there. If you want a shot at Michigan, you're going to have to play better than ever from here on out, day in, day out." He held open the door for Ken. "No more screwups, Ken. There won't be a second chance."

melissa Fox

I just watched <u>Titanic</u> again. It's a great movie and everything, but there's one thing I just don't get—that whole self-sacrifice thing. Sure, it's romantic and all, but I'm sorry—if I was in the water with a bunch of drowning people and there was one seat in the lifeboat, they could all just forget about it. There's no way I'd go down with a sinking ship.

CHAPTER

What Matters

12

Where do they find these people? Will wondered, his eyes fastened to the television screen. Today's topic on the talk show was "Husbands Who Let Their Wives' Boyfriends Move In." The guests were even more pathetic than usual. And he should know—he'd been watching a million of these shows. They were the only shows on during the day, aside from soap operas and infomercials.

He frowned as one man launched into an explanation of why he tolerated the fact that his wife's unemployed boyfriend had been staying in their guest room for three months. Were these people for real?

Then the host announced that another surprise guest was coming, and the audience was howling so hard, he had a hard time catching who she was. Whoa—he hadn't seen that one coming. Will chuckled to himself. The *husband's* girlfriend! As soon as the woman came onto the stage, the wife jumped up and went after her. The wife was a big woman too—it took three security guys to keep them apart.

Will put the television on mute, watching them wave around their arms in silence. It was pretty depressing, actually. They were all such total losers.

Like I'm much better. He was the loser *watching* these people yell at one another. They should have an episode of one of these shows on people like him. People who really had zero lives.

He turned off the TV with an angry jab at the power button. No wonder Melissa had ditched him for Ken Matthews. He'd become totally pathetic. He glanced around his room, disgust filling his stomach. His schoolbooks were still in a big pile, gathering dust. The only thing he'd read all week was *TV Guide.*

Melissa had said something about how his knee injury didn't have to be the end of his life. Maybe she wasn't totally off base. All he'd done was mope around the house, becoming such a waste of space that his own girlfriend couldn't respect him.

Ex-girlfriend, he reminded himself. But he couldn't keep using her as an excuse. How could she not be repulsed by the way he'd been acting? She couldn't be any more revolted than he was.

He couldn't go on like this. Things had to change—now. Melissa might have totally betrayed him, but what he was doing was much worse. It was exactly like she said, as much as he hated to admit it—he'd just given up, letting things happen to him without even trying to fight back.

He grabbed the *TV Guide* and threw it into the trash can, then struggled to his feet. It was unbelievable how weak he'd let himself get. He'd only hurt his leg, but even the muscles in his arms were slack. He could have been doing upper-body exercises this whole time. For that matter, he was supposed to be exercising his leg too.

He hobbled over to his desk and lowered himself into a chair. Just that much effort and his muscles were shaking. He rummaged through the heap of papers: unread homework assignments, unopened get-well cards—and then he found it. He unfolded the referral his doctor had written for the physical therapist. He was supposed to go as soon as the swelling went down. His parents had wanted him to go last week, but he'd said he wasn't ready.

There had to be a phone number on here somewhere. There. He reached over and picked up his football-shaped phone, then dialed the number on the card.

The receptionist answered, but she put him on hold before he could say anything. As he waited, listening to the elevator music, he thought about everything Melissa had said to him. The way she'd looked at him, like he was done, finished. He could handle pain. He could handle hard work. Whatever it took to get him back in shape, he'd do.

Some stupid doctor had said he wouldn't be able to play football again. Doctors were proved wrong all the time. He wasn't just going back to school—he was going to make it back on the team.

Jeremy drove slowly down the road toward Big Mesa High. There was no reason to rush. He was on his way to "celebrate" all by himself. His parents had to go to his dad's work party, and he didn't even have a date anymore.

I guess I should be relieved about that, though. He reached down to flip the radio stations, searching for something upbeat. Yeah, it was lame having to show up to this dinner solo, but wasn't it better than a night of pretending to feel something he didn't?

He pulled into the Big Mesa parking lot and found a space much closer than he could usually get. It was strange being here at night like this. There were so few other cars in the parking lot, and the whole place just felt so *still*.

He turned off the engine and climbed out of the car, stretching his legs. He glanced down at himself, checking to make sure his dark gray double-breasted suit was all in order. He wasn't big on dressing up. It had taken him fifteen minutes to get his tie on correctly.

He strolled toward the front steps of the school, glancing down at his watch. Right on time. When he looked back up, he saw a girl standing by the steps. From the back it looked like . . . Jessica. His heart rate accelerated automatically, even though he knew it couldn't be her.

Still, he quickened his pace, walking up right behind her. She was wearing a sleeveless black dress that clung to her slim body, and the closer he got, the more impossible it was to tell himself he was hallucinating. He knew the curve of her back and the slope of her shoulders way too well by now.

"Jessica?"

She spun around and smiled when she saw him. But it was a strange smile—a *sad* smile somehow.

"What are you doing here?" he asked.

She frowned. "What do you mean?" she asked. "Jade told me . . ." She stopped, glancing over his shoulder. "Where is Jade?"

"She's not coming," he said, his voice tight.

"Why not? Did something happen with her mother?" Jessica's eyes filled with concern.

"No, no, her mom's fine." He licked his lips nervously. "Actually, we, uh, broke up."

Jessica's eyebrows shot up. "What? But I thought you two were so—so happy together." She averted her eyes, and he wondered if he was crazy to think that she really *didn't* want him to be with Jade.

"No, we weren't," he began.

"Oh." She paused. "So, what about my date?" she asked.

Jeremy blinked, feeling like someone had just thrown a glass of ice water in his face. "Your date?"

he said. How many times did he have to be re-minded? She'd broken up with him once already. She wasn't interested.

"Yeah, my date. What's his name anyway?"

What was she talking about? She was meeting some other guy from Big Mesa and she didn't even know the guy's name?

"You know—the guy I'm meeting here tonight," Jessica continued. "Jade said—"

"Wait a minute," he interrupted. "Jade told you to meet a date here?"

"Yeah," Jessica said, looking at him like he was crazy. "For *you*. She said something about a friend who really needed a date and that if I came here, I'd be . . ." She trailed off, her whole expression changing. "She promised I'd be happy I showed up," she finished softly.

Suddenly Jeremy felt dizzy, as if everything had just turned upside down. "When exactly did Jade tell you this?" he asked.

"Right after practice."

So that whole fight had been a setup. Jade had planned it all out in advance—she knew he'd get mad if she flirted with Trent. She knew he wanted to be with Jessica, not her. And she'd made it happen.

"I can't believe it," he muttered. He glanced back at Jessica. Her blue-green eyes were more beautiful than ever in the soft moonlight. "Jess, do you realize what's going on here?"

She nodded. "She set us up," she said. "She must think that we . . . belong together."

"Yeah, I guess so," he agreed. He took a step closer to her. "And the truth is, I think so too," he said, staring into her eyes, finally letting himself feel everything he'd pushed away for so long now. It was overwhelming—a tidal wave of emotions so strong, he didn't know how he'd managed to hold them back. "So the question is . . . what do you think?"

Jessica looked up into Jeremy's open, trusting face, amazed at what she saw there. It was everything she'd wanted, everything she'd convinced herself would never be possible.

"Well . . . do you think she's right?" he asked.

His throat was so dry, she wasn't sure if she could speak. "Yeah, I do," she said. She started to smile, and suddenly she couldn't stop. Her lips broke into a wider grin than ever before, stretching out across her face.

He seemed confused at first, and then he smiled too. The smile turned into a laugh, and she joined him. They stood there giggling together until he grabbed her in his arms and pulled her against him.

The second his lips met hers, an explosion of absolute bliss went off inside her. He tightened his grip around her, and it was like every part of them was fused together completely.

They broke from the kiss, but Jeremy still clasped

her in his arms. "You know that feeling you have when you get off a roller coaster?" he asked, breathless. "How your whole body feels alive, and you're excited and laughing, and you just want to get back on and do it again? That's how I feel right now. I swear, I'm tingling all over."

"Tickets, please," Jessica said, and she pulled him toward her for another long, delicious kiss.

"Wow. I'm actually dizzy," Jeremy said when she let go. He leaned his head against hers, and Jessica could feel his warm breath on her neck.

She tucked a curl of black hair behind his ear, then traced the outline of his ear with her forefinger until he laughed. "Why didn't you tell me this was what you wanted?" she asked.

"I don't know," he said. "Why didn't you tell me?"

"You had a girlfriend, remember?" Jessica said. "Or did you forget about her?"

"How could I, when you kept trying to make me work things out with her? What was that all about anyway?"

Jessica felt a pang of regret. "I just wanted you to be happy, Jeremy. And I thought you would be, with her."

He smiled. "Well, next time you want to make me happy, I know a much better way. Just do this."

His lips touched hers again, and Jessica forgot about talking. It was like a knot had been untied inside her and all the feelings she'd kept bundled up in a tense little ball were loosening, unwinding, *finally*.

"Mmmm," Jeremy said, nuzzling her ear.

She sighed happily. "What do you think made her do that?" she asked him.

"Who?" he murmured.

"Jade."

Jeremy stepped back, narrowing his eyes. "I have no idea," he said. "What do you think?"

"I was just thinking—as long as I kept fighting, she fought back. And when I finally stopped, she did . . . this." She leaned her head against his chest. "Do you think that means something?"

"Definitely. It means you think too much." He kissed the top of her head.

"Jeremy? Shouldn't we go inside?" She smiled up at him. "I don't want them to give all your prizes to somebody else."

"Hey, I've already got what matters," he said, squeezing her.

She laughed, socking him gently on the shoulder. "Not if you keep throwing out cheesy lines like that one," she teased. But she knew he meant it, and now that they were back together—they both had everything they needed.

KEN MATTHEWS
7:18 P.M.

Calm down, Matthews. Everything's cool.

Michigan was never a sure thing anyway. A few weeks ago you weren't even starting, remember? And don't forget those five TDs last week. Even if Michigan falls through, you'll get in somewhere good. Don't let this get to you.

You're playing great, you're healthy, and you're the starting QB on an undefeated team. And you've got a good thing going with Melissa.

So how come when I came out of Riley's office today, all I wanted to do was call Maria?

JADE WU

7:22 P.M.

Well, no angry telephone calls from Big Mesa. They would have called by now if they were really mad.

So I guess they're in there right now. Probably holding hands, or gazing into each other's eyes, or whatever people in love do. Pretty nauseating.

But I still wish it was me.

JEREMY AAMES

7:27 P.M.

I really underestimated Jade. It took a lot of guts to do what she did. She told the truth, something I was having way too much trouble doing. I still can't believe Jessica's really here, right across the table, looking almost as happy as me.

Almost. Because it's just not possible for anyone to be as happy as I am right now.

JESSICA WAKEFIELD

7:28 P.M.

Mmmm...

Check out the **all-new**....

..... Sweet Valley Web site—

www.sweetvalley.com

New Features

Cool Prizes

The **ONLY** official Web site!

Hot Links

And much more!